D0497591

Love, sex and dating, the daily grind of work in Future Digital, being the other woman, the other man, Beauty and the Beast retold, rabbits, rats and foxes… In *Only the Visible Can Vanish*, Anna Maconochie brings tales of transformation and hidden identity, revealing the superficiality and depths of life in the internet age.

❧

Anna Maconochie was born in London, where she now lives and works. She has had stories published in the *Erotic Review*, the *Dublin Review* and the *Bitter Oleander*. This is her first short story collection.

Only the Visible Can Vanish is a looking-glass exploration of love, sex and dating: everything here is reflected, refracted, reversed. We are never far away from the fairytale. Anna Maconochie reveals herself to be a fresh and surprising new voice.

Betty Herbert, author of *The 52 Seductions*

If good writing through the ages either addresses, or puts across, or both, the unbearable fact of our aloneness, then Anna's work is great. It's also now, and very, very funny.

Kira Jolliffe, founder of *Cheap Date* magazine and co-founder/editor of *FANPAGES*

Sharply observed, seductive, slightly eerie, these stories take us beyond the familiarity of contemporary city life to stranger places; sometimes only a room away, sometimes a quantum leap... Maconochie's writing is also terrific fun.

Jamie Maclean, Editor, *Erotic Review*

To my parents

Only the Visible Can Vanish

Contents

Imposters

Fiona noticed the TV actor – successful, but not stratospherically famous – as soon as she and Millie entered the café. It was Sunday, nearly midday. The actor, in his gym gear, was seated in the far corner. Discipline, thought Fiona, discipline had got him where he was in life and now, post-workout, he was sipping a wholesome smoothie and spreading butter on a single piece of brown toast. He seemed to do everything just so, in no special hurry, and his chair and table were somehow like props, with their own special energy. His gaze appeared focused on the tall algae-coloured drink but she thought she could perceive his eyes scoping the terrain.

'Four o'clock,' she said to Millie as soon as they were seated.

'Who?' said Millie, irritated. They'd been discussing something deeply private, and Fiona thought Millie appeared jangled by the sudden shift in conversation. With the slowest turn of her head, Millie trained her eyes on the

1

actor.

'Cato Malone,' said Fiona.

'Cato who?'

'Keep your voice down,' Fiona hissed. 'You know. From *Long in the Tooth*. That American show about the old peoples' home where the old geezers are all vampires. He plays the struggling novelist who takes the night shift and discovers their secret.'

'Haven't seen it.'

'It's brilliant. Cato's amazing in it. He's quite cute, really. A bit nerdy and boyish, not a leading man exactly, but he sort of grows on you.'

'Get his autograph then.'

'Nah.'

'Better than asking for a selfie together. They hate that.'

'Why would I ask for anything at all from him?'

'So you get to talk to him.'

'Can't be arsed.'

'You're the one who said he was cute.'

'Pfffff.'

But Millie was getting curious. 'So he's American? What's he doing here?'

'He's British. I think he lives around here. He's just playing American. Brit actors come cheap.'

'It doesn't sound like a British name. Or even a real name.'

'It *is* his real name.' Fiona knew this from a careful read of an interview somewhere. 'It's Roman. Cato the Elder, Cato the Younger and all that.'

'I dare you to approach him,' said Millie. 'I dare you, Miss Classical Education.'

The actor, who had not been to the gym but was in fact hungover and dressed in a slightly tea-stained grey tracksuit, hastily plucked from his dirty washing basket due to a backlog of laundry that refused to dry in the perennial damp of his flat, had not wanted to get out of bed. The London Film School short he was supposed to be acting in today (for what the producer referred to as 'token payment', which felt oddly even worse than working for just expenses) had been postponed at the last minute. His Sunday was now a wasteland of unsought freedom. Having realised that morning that there was nothing in the fridge he could stomach after his unplanned bender the night before – drinks with a couple of old friends that should have been fun but somehow had left him bored and antsy – he had frogmarched himself into the café. Now he knew it had been a mistake. He was sure people were staring at him, which led him to curse himself for being so paranoid and hungover. The spirulina-shot smoothie – the ideal hangover cure, according to one of his friends from last night – tasted rank and bitter, but it had cost nearly four quid, so he had to drink it.

There was something familiar about the blonde girl chatting animatedly to another girl diagonally across the cafe. Could it be Lydia Carpenter? He'd met her only once, when he'd had a few lines in *Surgeons*, a year or more ago now. Lydia was big time now – *Downton Abbey*? Or was it *Game of Thrones*? He was pretty sure it was *Game of Thrones*. Some scheming princess. He almost got his phone out to check on IMDb but then decided he couldn't be bothered. He was in no state to approach Lydia Carpenter. A shame. She'd been so nice to him. She was nice to everyone, but she'd chosen to sit with him for lunch on the dining bus that shoot day. She could have sat anywhere else – with the director if she'd wanted. She'd given him so much encouragement; told him he had something. He'd wondered in retrospect whether she was flirting with him. She was a prankster, too, he remembered that. Whoopee cushion under one of the cameramen just as he sat down to eat. Knock-knock jokes. Ten different accents in one day. He wished more people were fun like that. She made you feel like everyone had it in them, they just had to let it out. As the weeks went by after that day on *Surgeons*, he'd wondered about getting in touch, seeing her again for coffee in a friendly way, one professional to another. And then he'd forgotten all about her when he'd met Michelle, and gone out with her for a few months, moved in with her, and then had one of shittiest break-ups of his whole life three weeks ago. Now, he was in no state to see Lydia. *How are you? What are you working on?* He was constructing answers to those questions in his head but he knew he couldn't face it.

Except now Lydia was walking over to him. Unstoppable, smiling, her blonde waves bouncing in a sort of perfect mess. He hadn't remembered her being so tall. He was trying not to notice her, not to look. As she got closer he remembered now she had a plainness, a blank quality to her face, perhaps noticeable to him only now as he'd never seen that face so still with intent. And yet she was beautiful, wasn't she? She had slightly hooded eyes. A bit sexy, almost sleepy. Very different from the big-eyed girls he normally went for, practically the opposite of Michelle's wide panicky blue ones. She was right here now, standing over him. Lydia. He looked up and met her face. He had no choice. It was Lydia but she looked slightly different. It struck him that some people always look like themselves, as if built each day from the same kit and others had faces that changed all the time. Was he just a little deflated by her somehow? God, no! He smiled and said hi, but still felt too hung over to jump up. Today of all bloody days.

'Hi,' she answered with a nervous smile. Then she handed him a gas bill from her red leather handbag and a ballpoint pen. He was so surprised he didn't say anything.

'Look,' she said. 'I don't have anything else for you to sign. But I'd love your autograph. My friend dared me,

I'm afraid. Would you do me the honour?'

Gone was Lydia's West Country accent – she was doing a London voice. She was pulling his leg. But she was bigging him up too. It was her way of saying *you are on to great things*. Hadn't she said something about practising his autograph on their day together? He took the gas bill from her and signed his name with a flourish while making sure it was legible – Simon Daly-Jones – and handed the bill and pen back to her. She studied the signature and he watched the deep-set eyes widen. She looked at him, blinking, as if in sudden bright light. He couldn't take the gag any longer.

'God, Lydia, you're good. You're totally freaking me.'

'Lydia?' Not-Lydia stared at him as if thick glass had sprung up between them. 'Am I going mad? You're not Cato Malone, are you? God, you look a lot like him! I'm so sorry, you must get this all the time.'

Simon let out a sigh. This was the third time he'd been mistaken for Cato Malone this year. The sodding oldies vampire show. He'd even gone on tape for the part Cato got after his plucky little agent had pushed for him to be considered. Back when he'd still had an agent. 'Yeah, all the time.' He smiled. 'I'm an actor as well so my life's a constant reminder of his success and my lack of it.'

'Shit. I am so, so sorry.'

'It's OK. You can keep the autograph,' he bounced the tone of his voice up so he wouldn't sound sarcastic.

'But hang on, um…' the girl looked at his autograph again. '*Simon*. You thought I was someone else too.'

'You look a lot like Lydia Carpenter. The actress.'

'Who's she?'

'She's in *Game of Thrones*.'

Fiona had seen every episode of *Game of Thrones*. She couldn't remember anyone called Lydia Carpenter in the credits. She gave him a confused look.

He couldn't think of anything to say to that look. Plus

he hadn't even seen *Game of Thrones* yet.

'So who *are* you?' he said with a useless jocularity that reminded him of his own father.

'I'm Fiona,' she said. 'Fiona who doesn't act.' She didn't offer a hand to shake.

'I think I've got that disease,' he said. 'That one where you can't recognise faces properly, even those of your own relatives. Proso – proso-something. Bollocks, I know I know this –'

'Well, thanks for the autograph, Simon,' Fiona said, with a winning smile, backing tentatively away. 'I'll keep it forever.'

'Can't say you'll get much for it on eBay.'

Fiona threw him a quick final wink as if to wrap things up and headed back to her table. Simon decided to stare at his smoothie, which was now confirmed as the only safe place in the world he could look. He had drunk an inch of it. A pound an inch, that was pretty much what it cost. He didn't want to finish it but he was going to. He couldn't leave it. By the time he dared look up from the drink Fiona was chatting away with her friend, sitting a little too far to the left to be comfortable, he thought. She must be hiding from him. Both of them were trying not to laugh, he could tell. They were holding the laughter in their bodies but it showed in the glimpses he caught of their faces, now pink with the effort of restraint.

His mind flashed over the possibility of wandering up to Fiona, retrieving the situation, telling her it was all OK, maybe he could even say he'd missed signing his middle initial and he could take back the gas bill and write his phone number on it instead. Why the hell not? She was cute. She was a nice person. He was sure of that. What were the odds of mutual misidentification? What a meeting story they'd have if they got together! He'd been to a movie première once, felt that odd sense of everyone and no one being a somebody, everyone caring and not caring where their gaze fell. Your brain couldn't keep up. But if you were Cato Malone, you probably just slotted right in. All he had to do was get up right now. She and the friend were starting to leave. They'd been here no more than twenty minutes – were they leaving because of him? He had to move now. Act like he was leaving at the same time as them. That wouldn't be weird, would it? But the smoothie. He couldn't leave the bloody smoothie, not at that price. And it would look suspicious. His brain couldn't get round the drink. He had to finish it. It was too much to down in one. He'd probably throw up. It didn't taste that bad, at least not as bad as the first few sips. He looked away from the girls busying themselves with their coats and bags and scarves and stared into the thick goo, the slowly swirling green layers like fat tendrils of smoke in endless caress, the thousands of minuscule granules that he couldn't individually trace no matter how much his tongue searched for them.

Derma

She's still at work even though it's past seven. She just showered in the cubicle in the ladies' toilets, and now she's sipping a glass of white wine at her desk, away from the party. She snuck up there before anyone else and poured herself a big one while the other P.A.s were still at their desks. He's there now, doing whatever it is he has to do. She'd rather leave him to it. He can miss her.

Except he doesn't leave it long enough. He comes bustling out of the lift, the ones that play radio stations, leaving a trail of pop music in the hallway as the doors open and close. He looks worried as usual.

'What are you doing at your desk? Why aren't you at the drinks?' he asks her.

There's no one around so he sits down next to her on a swivel chair and kisses her. The rhythm of his kiss brings to her mind a mobile phone being plugged in to charge, the battery sign endlessly emptying and filling.

'You smell amazing,' he says. 'Like cedar wood.'

'Disco,' she says. 'I just showered.' She points to the tub of cedar wood moisturiser she keeps next to her computer screen. The lid's calligraphic letters promise to relieve her of all stress, to take her into a cedar forest just by rubbing her hands.

'You going somewhere fun tonight, Miss Clean?'

'No, I just felt like a shower. I wanted to vanish and turn into water,' she says.

'They want me back up there,' he says, looking forlorn.

She doesn't say anything. She picks up her glass of wine and walks into his office, the one he has been allocated strictly for private meetings. Not even she gets to sit in there, even though she's his primary assistant – her desk is outside. He follows her. They face each other, and she undoes his belt-buckle, and then gestures to him to undo the rest while she removes the silver cat's head brooch pinning her shirt closed at the neck. He puts his hand down inside her underwear. She pauses for a moment and then does the same to him. No one can see them, no one would dare come into his office without knocking, but there's still a part of her that fears being discovered. Except there's nothing to discover. They all know and they don't seem to care. She gets there faster than expected. Through a slight kink in the drawn metal blind she can just about see a cleaning trolley minus a human dozens of metres away and she reaches for her wineglass and takes a gulp. He's the one lagging behind, even though he's always ready from the get-go, despite having to be one floor above, shaking someone's hand.

Finally he gives up.

'I'd better get cleaned up,' he sighs. 'You OK? You need anything?'

She watches him go off to wash his hands. His legs are long and thin, making her think of saplings, wheat growing tall. Suddenly she longs for the fir trees where she grew up in Colorado, not this lone island of cloned buildings in this huge tangled city. London. A city she chose a long time ago for a different man and a job she chose for the money.

'I'll see you up there?' he says.

'In a minute, Boss.'

'Do you have to call me that?'

She gives him a stare as he leaves.

By 5am she can't sleep so she simply gets up and goes to work. When she arrives, the sky is still dark blue, almost violet, the same shade as when she left yesterday and for some reason her wine glass is still on her desk, with its red lipstick print. The office is empty. She could trick herself or someone else into believing she never left yesterday night, like the last ten hours have been edited out. Now she's here, she wishes it was evening and she could go home. She's so tired she feels nauseous, like she has jetlag. She feels a pull towards the bathroom, the urge to shower and examine her skin, but she's already had one this morning, and she heard a radio voice in the lifts on the way up talking about how parts of England are now as dry as East Africa. She pictures an expanse of hard cracked earth, fissures, lone weeds prevailing.

A few hours later, the other two assistants in her section arrive and settle at the island of desks and computers they all share. Both fortyish blondes with bad dye jobs. She wishes she could just tell them. Lose a stone, dye it back to brown. She wishes they could just tell her too, but she knows what they would say.

The slightly younger one has a little girl, and talks about the girl's father like he's an employee she shouldn't have hired. The older woman is alone but she's 'ready', she says with a smile, like she's about to do a cartoon high dive into a barrel of water far below.

When she was promoted to executive assistant it felt like she was alone with him all the time, even when they weren't in the same room, but now she just feels alone. People leave their jobs every week in this office, saying goodbye via mass email, inviting everyone for a beer. The whole place feels past tense. There is talk of the building complex being sold, but it is so big she wonders who could buy even one of the buildings. There is a designated social area every hundred metres, like emergency exits on a plane, with sofas and plants and coffee stations. There is one station that has a real plant, not a fake like the others. Something tropical she can't place. She is used to mountain plants and trees, not palms and cacti that remind her of the California desert where her mother now lives. The cleaners dust the leaves every night. The plant is the size of a tree but with the build of a plant. It makes her feel miniature. She touches it every single time she walks past.

'Martha,' the older blonde says. 'Martha, how did you meet your other half?'

'Gary? Oh, we met when we were teenagers. Kept getting smashed together at the same parties.'

'Ah.'

Their conversations are always like that, like a stone being thrown across the water in that particular way so it will bounce three times before it sinks. The older woman is always the one throwing the stone. When he's not around, she tries to salvage these conversations, so she turns to the older blonde and says: 'Why don't you and I go for a drink? See if we can't chat up a fella or two.'

'Really?'

'Even if there's no one, it'll still be fun.'

'I thought you had someone,' the older blonde replies.

'No,' she says, voice staccato. 'I don't.'

The next day a giant plume of smoke billows up over all

the buildings. It is so thick it is easy to see where the smoke ends and the air begins. She likes this neatness, this definition. There's a nearby plastics depot on fire, she reads on Twitter. She reads about the unholy stench, the spreading blame. There's no emergency drill sounding despite all the practice drills they've done during the year. She feels an itch on her shoulder. A mole? No, a whitehead blown up from nowhere. This job, she thinks.

People get up to take pictures on their phones of the buildings dwarfed by the smoke so they don't see her dark grey coat with its fake fur collar slither off her chair and glide away, levitating a foot above the floor, nearly invisible against the grey carpet. Grey on grey until it turns beige, then russet, then grows legs and a head and a tail. It is a large male fox. It meanders slowly down the long wide hallway past the new toffee-coloured wooden walls. She watches. The vertical wood panels blister as if restraining a fire, then darken, green sprouting up and out through bark, green upon green, at first with the flatness of a theatre set, then endlessly thick. The fox heads towards it.

'Come back,' she cries, getting up and following it. The fox turns its head for a moment and grins, yellow eyes flat as glass. It turns away and vanishes into the deepening forest. She returns to her desk. 'Jeez, you look like you've seen a ghost,' the blondes both tell her at the same time. 'Have a Treat,' says the younger one, offering her a piece of chocolate like a small brown pebble.

'I want to see you,' says her boss that afternoon when they are in his office getting started, her stockinged foot creeping up his trouser leg. 'I want to go slow this time. I don't have to be anywhere this afternoon. We're always rushing. You never let me see you.'

'No,' she says, 'you're the one who always has to rush off.'

'Please let me see you.'

'You're seeing me now,' she says.

'You know what I mean.'

It's been six months but he's never seen her fully naked. Their affair hasn't even left the office. He barely leaves it himself, and when he does, he leaves in a majestic way. Dubai, Australia, Singapore. She doesn't think he's even touched her in full daylight.

'OK,' she says. 'You asked for it.'

She takes everything off without his assistance and folds it quickly like she's in an examining room. Then she stands very still, facing him. From the undersides of her breasts to just above her knees are red marks interspersed with whitish scars from the spots she has continuously aggravated and even welts fussed up from practically nothing. He has felt some of them directly with his hands before but seeing them is different from feeling them, she knows that much. The flat scars are pale and smooth. In certain lights they look like tiny plastic inserts, like the circles that fly off when she holepunches his meeting agendas in their plastic folders.

'Christ,' he says.

She stares at him.

'You're not well,' he mumbles, grasping for words. 'You should take some paid leave. As of now. I'll get the department to cover it.'

'How about the department covers a cosmetic dermatologist?' she asks.

'Whatever,' he says.

An hour later, after he has left, she goes for a walk. People are always telling her it's good to do that. Plus her coat is still missing. There is a lot you can do to find lost things here, online forms, mass emails to the right distribution lists. There's even a lost property department. She can walk this office for a rectangular mile without leaving it.

But when she gets back her coat is on the back of her chair as usual. It's warm all over. Did a very overheated person borrow it? Unlikely. She strokes the furry collar a little as if it might yield an answer. Then it happens. She doesn't talk but words leave her silently like a scent and she knows they are received. Doing it is instinctive, like a talent she knows everyone has but feels unique when you first use it.

I thought you'd left me. I thought you were gone in that forest forever.

A moment passes and new words are volleyed back.

How could I ever leave you? There is nothing in this world as lovely as you and never will be. Meet me in the bathroom in five minutes.

Oh. OK, sure.

There is no one in the ladies' when she goes in. She's not afraid exactly, but she's wired – on edge – so she goes to the centre of the room. There is something safe about the centre of a room, she is convinced. Away from the corners. Things lurk in corners. If there is inescapable danger, it will find you quickly in the centre and then the end is hastened. So she stands right in the middle of the room letting the fluorescent light illuminate her. She wants to say *where are you?* but she can't get it out, she's already lost the knack. Then a very tall red-haired young woman in rags comes out of the nearest cubicle. There are dark stains on the rags and her body. She bends over and the rags turn to fur, covering the bare skin, the arms turn to front legs and she is a fox. It skulks around in a semi-circle and grins, staring at her the whole time, licking its teeth, working its long jaws.

'What are you?' she says out loud. She has to say the words so she knows all this is real and she is not talking to fox-coloured air in her mind.

This is the real me. The fox doesn't talk but if it had a voice they'd be a man's words. She doesn't hear. She absorbs. The force of the silent words is strong enough to knock her over but it doesn't.

'I had to turn human briefly to get in the bathroom. Too many people around outside,' says the fox.

'Oh. Right.'

'You have something at the top of your left shoulder blade. Something that wants to come out. Badly. Does it itch?'

'Yes,' she says.

'I'd get it out for you,' the fox says. 'But not with these paws and teeth. So you must get it out. Do you want me to watch?'

'Yes,' she says. 'I would like that. I can't see it properly, even with these mirrors everywhere.'

'I promise no one will come in here,' says the fox.

'OK'.

'Take off your shirt.'

'You promise no one will come in here?'

'Time has slowed right down,' says the fox. 'I can wrap an hour in the skein of a second.'

Carefully she removes her white work shirt, placing it next to the sinks, hoping it won't get wet.

'You're even lovelier without your shirt on. All that bare skin. It's so bright, I can hardly look.'

She plucks a paper towel from the dispenser on the wall by the sink, places it on standby, pulls her bra strap off her shoulder and pinches the skin up as far as she can to see the spot. The contortion crescendos in pain as she closes in.

'Squeeze harder, says the fox. Get it all out. That stuff is voodoo.'

'How do you know?'

'You humans store your misery in a thousand ways.'

'What makes you think I'm miserable?'

'Observing how content you are now. You have blood coming out of your shoulder. Get down on the floor and I'll clean you up.'

She folds her legs and sits on the cold blue floor. This makes her feel like an animal, relating to the world from a low, horizontal place, her eyes meeting the fox's eyes at the same level until she turns her back to give him her shoulder. He approaches her slowly and then licks her whole shoulder, licks the tiny cavity she has made. Delicious, he says. He seems expert at whatever it is he is doing, she can feel in his tongue strokes the years of fighting, crunching, gripping like a vice to the death. Then stripping meat off the bone, ripping through tissue and membrane. Her shoulder feels nice now. When she looks in the mirror there's just a neat puncture where his tongue has been, where her long nails bit the skin. She takes a sharp breath.

'I know what you're thinking,' says the fox. 'But I don't love you in the way that makes me want to kill you.'

'Does that mean you love all the rabbits and chickens you've…'

'Oh yes. I love them more than they can ever know. But not in a way you would understand. And not like how I love you.'

'I love you too. I love you so much.'

The fox looks at her and she realises she was mistaken, not in how much she is loved by him but how that love shows on his face. Of course the face of a fox does not have the same readable expressions as a human face. He grins simply to bare his predatory teeth, not to allude to anything between them that excites him. Now his eyes look sad when they meet hers but she doesn't know what to think. In his world, which might be quite different from her world, sadness could be the feeling that is craved the most.

'I want to ask you something.'

'Anything, Beautiful.'

'Tell me about that forest you went into,' she says.

'You saw it for yourself,' says the fox. He cocks his head to one side.

'Can you take me there?'

He shakes his head. There is no doubt what he means by that.

When she returns to her desk the blondes eye her tenderly, tell her they are sorry she has to take time off. 'We're not here to judge,' they say. 'As long as you take the time to go through whatever it is you're going through. Let me make you a cup of tea,' the older one says. 'Don't pack up just yet.'

'Thank you,' she says, 'but first I need a shower.'

Something huge is in store for her, for certain. She can't fully feel it yet, but she knows it's coming.

If Not Yourself, Who Would You Be?

Molly and Isaac decided to meet for their first date at a newly opened diner-style bar/restaurant in Islington. It wasn't an all-out Americana tribute, but it had proper dining booths that offered privacy without too much intimacy. It was a good choice for a first date, Molly thought, because you could order food and drink at will – lunch at four, cocktails at noon, or even breakfast for dinner. It had been Isaac's fairly insistent suggestion they meet there, but Molly had read a sterling review of the place in *Time Out* and their agreement on venue made her feel reassured, if not outright excited about meeting him.

Molly was thirty-four, saw herself as something near pretty, and at the point in life where her capacity for having fun (as well as having more ready cash to spend on fun) had increased in conjunction with her decision to approach finding a long-term boyfriend, or even husband, like a proper project. Looking back on her twenties, she was amazed at how earnest she had been, how much less she had drunk, chanced, experimented. Certainly she wouldn't have considered internet dating back then, nor would she have found the courage to walk into a restaurant, smile at someone she had never met in person and even kiss them on the cheek on arrival, as was *de rigueur* amongst internet daters these days it seemed (or at least in her brief experience). The Molly she remembered being a decade ago was someone who got hung up, sometimes for years at a time, on what her mother called 'unsuitable choices' or what her best friend Freya called 'fey gays.' 'Those fake rock stars don't fancy you,' Freya would say. 'You're just not their species. And, besides, they're all gay, really, aren't they – all those narcissistic chest-waxing gym-bunny Hoxtonites.' Freya knew these things because they fancied *her* plus her capacity for danger.

Extricating her emotions from the unsuitable, Molly had found, required considerable effort, and yet another effort was needed to retrain those well-worn hopes on the potentially promising, the ones she might have missed. But now, after a perfectly acceptable, if less than thrilling, year-long relationship with James, a web developer, that had ended with a slow glide into friendship, she felt ready. On New Year's Day she stuck herself first on a free dating site, then later in January she chose one with a monthly subscription – the fee irritating her into genuine pro-activeness. Three months later, Isaac wrote to her on Guardian Soulmates and they began messaging about his PhD thesis on feminist views of post-millennium semantics.

Isaac had arrived early, texting her to let her know he was at the back, and asking what drink she would like? When she found the corner booth he had selected, an overly-garnished Bloody Mary was waiting for her. They greeted each other with decided friendliness, locked eyes for a second, and Molly thought what she couldn't help thinking on every internet date, a thought that barely made it into words before being waved away like smoke in her mind. *I don't fancy you.* And then the instant boomerang. *Do I?*

'So…!' she said, the 'o' of 'so' breaking off into an extra syllable as she sat down with a jolt in their booth. The meat-coloured leather seat was plump yet strangely low. She sat upright, but the table still came up to just below her breasts.

'This place is exactly how I pictured it!' she said.

'I love it here,' said Isaac. 'They make any milkshake you want. I confess…' and he leaned conspiratorially towards Molly, 'I got here early so I could have a malt before you arrived. And now I'm having another.'

'Sweet tooth.'

'I don't know why I just told you that,' he exclaimed. 'You'll think I'm greedy.'

'Just a manly appetite.'

'Well … enough about me. Tell me about you. I want to know everything. How was your day? How's the guitar going?'

Molly smiled. 'You know plenty about me already.'

It was true. He knew things about her even James didn't know. She and Isaac hadn't spoken on the phone, but they had been emailing and instant messaging for nearly a month. Molly had had other conversations on both her sites with other men, some becoming regular, and two that had flourished into perfectly agreeable one-time dates, but she and Isaac had kept up throughout. He had decided they should both do Proust's questionnaire, the one celebrities used to do on the back page of *Vanity Fair*. This impressed her. *I remember when VF was a good magazine*, he had messaged almost at talking speed. If not yourself, who would you be? was his favourite question. He insisted they gender switch it. Mary Wollstonecraft for him. Paul Newman for her. *Yeah, that magazine's really gone to pot,* Molly had written, imagining that he must be taking the same kind of cosy delight in her retro turn of phrase as she was in agreeing with him that *Vanity Fair* was, like, so over. They used to both read *Vanity Fair*! They both still read *The New Yorker*!

'Sorry the seating's a bit low,' he acknowledged, as Molly leaned on the table. 'You must be worried I lied about my height. I'm six feet, I promise.'

From what she could see, he was bigger in person than she had anticipated, but only a little. In the 'body type' section on their site he had ticked 'a few extra pounds', and Molly was pretty certain she could see the top section of a broad but flattish beer gut, not that it bothered her. She had ticked 'curvy' on her own profile. When she recounted the whole night to Freya the next day, she admitted that in theory, despite the honesty of her profile pictures, he could have been a little surprised on seeing her for the first time. She had gained an additional fifteen pounds during her early thirties, and she was content with that. 'You have a great figure,' Freya always told her. 'Considering who you could get, you're not fussy enough.'

As she and Isaac settled into various overlapping threads of conversation and another round of drinks (he refused to let her pay, although he had her fetch the drinks, making her wonder each time what part or parts of her he might be checking out), Molly's discussion with herself continued to simmer. *I don't fancy you.* But as their evening together began to bloom into a good time, her mind created another debate: she wondered if there was a level of comfort that might serve as a foundation for something else between them. He was forty-one. It was evident he liked her. He seemed absolutely ready for a real girlfriend. Yet as Isaac started talking in depth about his PhD thesis, it was James she couldn't help thinking about, the sweet fizz of anxiety in her blood during the early days with him. James hadn't played any mind games with her, but in those early days she had felt every moment with him had been part of an unspoken assessment like a driving test. She took a long suck on her second Bloody Mary.

Isaac was now explaining something about syntax and semantics. She realised while she was thinking about James, she wasn't listening properly. *Focus,* she thought. He's actually quite handsome. I am on a date with a handsome man. Isaac's eyes were dark but they were a slightly paler brown than his near-black hair; a pleasing combination. His teeth were well-cared for. His face was a bit doughy, but she could trace the bones holding it up, creating an appealing stage on which his kindness and wit could act. I like this face, she thought. They really could talk, too. She worried sometimes that she was too talkative, especially with men, but with Isaac, one conversation just led to another. Next they were onto families. Her parents clinging on, trying to make do and not divorce. His sister's husband acting like a psycho, threatening to take his nephew away. Molly had told herself more than once not to be emotionally slutty on dates, not to reduce her own family's fragility into a mere topic of chat. What if he were to meet them someday? She had already killed the chance for it to dawn on him that her parents might not be happy people. It was just so hard to resist divulging.

'Well, that's just it, isn't it? We live in this highly therapised age,' Isaac concluded the latest strand of their conversation.

'I've resisted therapy thus far.'

'Therapy is the fashionable tonic of our era. However, while I don't see it as a cure-all, I do think it's useful.'

There was, for the first time, a dead moment between them. Molly wasn't really interested in therapy. In fact it made her feel a little uncomfortable with its growing cultural omnipresence. She was just about to fill the silence with something, anything, but then Isaac added: 'I'm pro-therapy but I do think people think too much. I hate intellectualising everything, actually. And I'm doing a PhD! And teaching semantics. Ridiculous, really. When it comes down to it, we are animals.'

The clichéd 'animals' comment, with its vague implications of sex, irritated Molly. Be specific if you're going to say something like that, she thought, even though she didn't really want him to be specific. Searching for a new subject, she stared at Isaac's houndstooth jacket. She decided it must be expensive as it had taken time for her to notice that it was quite daringly coloured as well as nicely made – a subtle burnt orange combined with faded indigo.

'Where'd you get your jacket?'

'Oh, a designer pal of mine made it for my fortieth.' Now he seemed cool – not just stylish, but remote. Molly was a paediatrician. She didn't have designer pals. But then he smiled at her and the cold vanished.

'Another round?' he asked.

She hesitated. She was all talked out. She realised she wanted him to take himself away, show her she could miss him, but it seemed he would only end their date at her command.

'I would, but I have an early start tomorrow.'

'Of course. Well, I'm going to stay here, maybe order one of their splendid burgers, so I'm sorry not to walk you out.'

'It's fine.'

Molly got up and started putting on her coat. Isaac watched her, still seated. She stood next to him, started to say goodbye as she did up the buttons and slung on her two bags. She felt flustered. Were they going to discuss meeting up again? She wanted to, didn't she? Out of habit, she checked her main bag to make sure everything was there, but it was half open, not fully on her shoulder and her scrabbling movements made something fall out. Her wallet. As if conspiring, her phone rang loudly. As she silenced it and adjusted her bags, she expected Isaac to shuffle over and pick up her wallet but he didn't. She picked it up herself, which involved crouching down with two heavy bags in high heels. As she rose, Isaac looked anxious.

'Everything OK?' she asked.

'Fine.'

The way he said 'fine' stung her a little. 'What's going on?' she asked him. 'Is it that I dropped my wallet? Were you worried I'd lose it?'

'No.'

This man has been sitting here, Molly thought, for nearly three hours straight. He hasn't been to the gents, he hasn't been to the bar. He got here before me and it seems he won't move until I'm gone.

'Isaac,' she said. 'You're a nice guy. But you didn't pick up my wallet. You ignored it. And now you seem upset. I don't mind you not picking up the wallet, I mean, it's not like there's some *law*, it's just…'

'I'm sorry.'

'It's fine, it's just… You haven't got up in three hours.'

'So?'

'So is there something I don't know? Like, can you stand up? Are you going to be OK leaving?'

'Sure,' he said. 'But I'm not getting up for you. I don't appreciate your tone.'

'Well, I don't like the way you seem to be hiding something from me.'

Isaac sighed. He didn't get up – he slid. Slowly towards her. He slid along the seat of the booth in preparation to maybe get up. When he finally did, she tried hard not to react. Below the ribs he was elephantine, bell-shaped like a compressed slug. His vast gut hung low over the widest hips she'd ever seen on a man. He shot her a look composed of rage and apology in equal measure.

Molly did something that later she would decide had been the only viable option. She turned and walked away.

Years later she would play detective with that night. Had he arranged for their booth to somehow have lower seating than the others? Was he planning to go six hours without urinating if necessary? What if she hadn't challenged him? Would she have seen him again, messaged with him into the night, sent him YouTube links on fanciful whim, unknowingly delaying the inevitable? She thought the Isaac story might morph into a good anecdote over time but it didn't. She did, however, try Proust's questionnaire with considerable success on her next internet prospect, a reforming Hoxtonite who showed up wearing the exact same jacket Isaac had worn. 'My lucky jacket,' Stanley said with a grin. 'Thirty quid in the H&M sale.'

The Real Beast

So it had been a year. So what? They'd had two children, one after the other, he was tired, she was tired. As they lay together each night in their vast horsehair-sprung bed, failing to fall easily asleep despite their constant weariness, and certainly not doing what they'd done a year ago when she'd been heavily pregnant and horny as hell, Bel regularly wondered what pre-meditated, not-in-the-mood-for-it sex would be like with her husband. Would she get in the mood? She was never in the mood for jogging, but once she started she often didn't want to stop, so intense was the endorphin kick. But *what if*, what if they put the babies down, knocked back some Chablis or even something stronger, unplugged the landline in case Gaenor, her witch of a sister, dared call past ten, and then, well, what if she just didn't get in the mood? Or he didn't? If it was mediocre for both of them, that would surely have proven a worse gamble than to have remained waiting for the auspicious moment, as they were unspokenly but complicitly doing. Or at least so Bel thought. It was just the right moment hadn't come.

She still fancied Jean-Louis, of course. Everyone fancied her husband. The American yoga-mommies here in South Kensington – they often flirted with him right in front of her. His French accent. The cresting waves of his thick black hair that played off so perfectly against the swell of his cheekbones. But the yummy and even not so yummy mummies, they thrilled at the unexpected too. His obsession with rose gardening, for example. So English, they remarked, even though Jean-Louis was always quick to point out his family had cultivated roses for centuries in France. His breezy lack of regret at losing the Le Comte family pile in Montargis (*Was it really a castle? Was his father really a Viscount?* Her nosier new friends had spent weeks pussyfooting around her fall from silly money to mere, well, money). He had no trouble telling whoever enquired that the *chateau* had had to be sold off, and they had decided to move to London, in part to be nearer Bel's ageing father, and get jobs like normal people. Well, he had found a passably normal job with BNP Paribas, a glorified starter gig really, whereas Bel, five months pregnant at the time with Aurore, their second, had finagled the sale of their wedding photos and 'hopping the channel' story to *Hello!* and then had gone begging to her former modelling agency, in the end settling on a contract with Pregnaglow.

It was all for the best, Jean-Louis always said. *C'est tout pour le mieux.* What he never revealed to anyone except Bel was how terrified he'd been of how she would react when he announced the quick sale of the estate. On receiving the news, she had simply smiled and said 'I'm pregnant again.' She thought he might collapse when she said those words, as if the timing were a joke to him, a curse even; the second baby a terrible gift, the one that would wreck everything. A gift he could not refuse. She knew he couldn't live with another curse again, not after escaping the one that had dominated his youth. A king is supposed to protect his queen from danger, he'd said. Yet Bel was calm about the future. She knew this wasn't how a wife, especially a newly pregnant one, was supposed to look when her husband told her he'd protect her. She was supposed to melt in his arms, not suppress a laugh. On seeing the crestfallen look in his eyes, she'd reassured him – of course she believed he could protect her. But what danger was there? She could live anywhere with him, take the babies anywhere he asked. He let out a great sigh. 'Actually,' he said, 'I'm happy to see the bloody palace go. It was so isolated, and that's the feeling I'll take from it, even though you came and transformed me from the outcast I used to be. I used to get lost in my own orchard. That bedevilled place was only going to fall into more debt and dry rot and brambles. Besides, London offers so many more opportunities, especially for the kids.'

'It's a real shame they won't grow up bilingual.' Bel said one night in bed as they were meandering in and out of conversation, trying to drift off.

This woke her husband right back up.

'Come on, they would have grown up illiterate in Montargis! They would have been spoilt monosyllabic brats who think everyone lives in a castle with tutors and a cook. There was no school for miles. At least here they get a taste of real life in a house with only one garden in a thriving metropolis. There are children from all over the world in South Ken.'

Bel couldn't resist laughing this time. She had watched her father bleed his fortune dry during her teens. Slowly they'd moved further out of London, first into a smaller house, then into a downward spiral of dingy flats; her sisters sharing a bunk, her on a sofabed she folded up each morning. Growing up, she had decided to be good with money. She had realised it was a decision, not a talent. The Pregnaglow contract was good timing, but the fee she got dwarfed her husband's starting salary at the bank. She was careful to squirrel away small but not too small sums into the kids' trust funds in hope of bringing the numbers down to a level that would reduce his embarrassment at having such a lower income figure on their joint bank statements.

'What's so funny?' Jean-Louis asked.

'Our house has four bedrooms. Four. "Only one garden"? You should hear yourself.'

'I know it's a rabbit hutch compared to France, but I'm really happy here.'

Bel grew quiet. I get lost in our house, she wanted to say. Sometimes I wake up in this very bed and wonder where I am.

'*Mon ange,* I almost forgot. Your sister called again.'

'Which one?'

'Gaenor.'

Bel groaned.

'Why don't you invite her over for brunch this weekend?' Jean-Louis said. 'I'll make pain perdu. She hasn't even met Aurore yet. You know you love her really.'

'Darling I could cheerfully strangle you sometimes.'

'Please!' said Jean-Louis, turning to face her. 'You are physically very powerful and I don't know who my wife is when she talks like that. I find it disturbing, actually.'

Bel caught her breath. 'I'm sorry darling, I won't do it again.'

I'd try the phrase 'sense of humour failure' on you, she thought. But you wouldn't find it funny.

When people asked how they had met, she would go *well, there's a tale,* and Jean-Louis' eyes would haze over with soppy adoration on cue like an actor. Except he wasn't acting. 'My father used to own several houseboats,' Bel would begin. 'Sadly, over the years, he had to sell them off to raise my two sisters and I. He was the sole parent as my mother died very young. By sixteen, I was modelling to pay off the family debts but that wounded my father's pride as he didn't want his youngest child to be the breadwinner. The last boat he still owned by the time I was nineteen was near Montargis, as he'd lived around there before we were born. He had rented it out to a friend for two decades but the friend moved to America, and when Dad went to recover the boat, it was completely rotted through. He had pinned his hopes on this boat as a final source of cash so, on seeing the ruined boat, discovering the so-called friend had abandoned it, he had a sort of on-the-spot crisis. A breakdown, even. He downed a bottle of whiskey, abandoned his rental car, passed out in a forest (the Le Comte Estate forest it turned out), woke up completely lost and was then found by one of Jean-Louis' gardeners who took him back to the chateau and pretty much brought him back to life. Jean-Louis made sure he was fed and doctored, but he was too shy to meet him.'

'Well,' Jean-Louis would interject. 'I was in such a state back then. Acute social anxiety since childhood.'

This blunt revelation always caught people off guard, but he never seemed to notice. He was always watching his wife whenever she told the story.

'So Dad stayed there a week and didn't meet Jean-Louis until he found him stealing a rose from the garden.'

'I was furious,' said Jean-Louis. 'It was part of the anxiety thing – I couldn't regulate my responses. I practically leapt on him. Then he explained, nearly in tears, that his daughter wanted a rose from France and he couldn't let her down. I thought, this man, he is completely crazy. But there's something about him I like. He's a romantic.'

Women always cooed at this point. The men tried not to squirm. Bel would hastily explain her father was always buying them presents to conceal his lack of money, and of course her older sisters, once they heard *France* were all like, bring on the foie gras and couture, whereas she had thought it would be nice just to get a rose, you know, all the way from France. She had no choice but to ask for some sort of gift from him, and this would cost little or nothing.

Someone would always ask if she still had the rose.

'Pressed and framed.' Jean-Louis would answer. 'It's on the mantelpiece next to our wedding photos. Take a look when you're next over with your kids.'

'So Jean-Louis gave Dad boxes of never-worn samples he'd been sent from Paris Fashion Week, as he used to sponsor that, and luckily they fit Gaenor and Regina well enough, and he told Dad he simply had to come back and visit him.'

'I liked her father a lot by then. Felt I'd made a friend for the first time.'

'Well, Dad felt the same. Plus he took "come back" as an order.'

'It *was* an order.'

Again the cooing and squirming. The collective sense of 'what's wrong with this picture?' that Bel couldn't always pick up but found herself looking for more and more. She couldn't tell anymore if she was drawing it from her audience or if they were catching it off her. This is how it really happened, she always wanted to say. I'm not making it up.

'So a few months later, Dad decides to go back and my sisters and I are all, like, who is your rich mystery pal in France, and why can't we come? And Dad's all cagey-like, my friend wants to see me alone and we're like, have you gone *gay*? Anyway, his hernia operation came up for the week he had planned to go back, so he asked Jean-Louis if I could go instead.'

'I was disappointed, but I agreed,' Jean-Louis would say. 'Of course when I actually laid eyes on Isabel, I thought, I must have this girl in my life forever. She will redeem me. I don't know how, but she will.'

'I stayed for five months.' Bel would continue. 'There's something timeless and engulfing about that part of France. It sucks you in, almost makes you forget your former life. I fired my modelling agency after the first month. Straight after that he asked me to marry him.'

'She kept saying no. I tried every trick in the book. You know, get her drunk, snuggle on the chaise-longue, read to her, throw in the line "will you marry me?" mid-sentence.'

'I'd be like, why did Aramis just say that to D'Artagnan? Show me that page!'

'I even embroidered MARRY ME on a napkin so she'd stumble upon it in the breakfast room.'

'I refused every time. I was like, I'm nineteen! I didn't think he was serious half the time. Also, after a while, I realised how homesick I had become, so I said I was going back to London for a week. He threw a fit.'

'I'll admit I was a little over-possessive.'

'He said only if I went in his helicopter and Skyped him every night at…'

'Nine pm British time, ten pm French time.' They always chanted this bit together.

'So we Skyped every night,' Bel would say, 'Except it was kind of awkward as I was always out at a restaurant or a party and the least noisy place was usually the toilet and he would be like *why are you always in the bathroom?* and I'd be like, I'm at some insane fashion party and he'd go, *I'm so lonely I just played chess with myself and made up the moves you could have played* and I'd feel so guilty. But I was having fun, so I decided to stay an extra night in London, and when we Skyped that night, I noticed his eyes were all red and he was shaking, and I was like, did you forget your pills?'

'I was on these herbal supplements to help with the anxiety but they were quite strong. So I go, *merde*, I forgot to take them because I'm all over the place as I miss you so much.'

'And I'm like, why are you outside in the rose garden in the rain, you weirdo, you'll get even sicker!

'The roses reminded me of her.'

'So I said, look, I'm getting on a plane *now*, and he said, I already sent Guillaume with the helicopter. It just landed on your street.'

One of the divorced mothers had quietly started sniffling at this, Bel remembered.

She frequently had to tell the story (and the more times she told it, the more it began to feel like a story, rather than intimate events in her own very real life) as all they seemed to do was meet people, their eyes like saucers, who wanted a golden droplet of what they had. Pregnaglow people, Jean-Louis' Paribas colleagues, other parents, au pairs, nursery teachers, Pilates teachers. Their lawyer, their accountant, her personal trainer, you name it – everyone wanted to know where this pair of awfully nice young ubermensches had landed from. The dinner party cycle, the playdate invites rallying back and forth – just thinking about the social planning involved in keeping everything ticking over made her feel tired. She had worried that after his solitary life in France, Jean-Louis wouldn't be able to cope with the stream of new faces, but now she found his unexpected assurance at mingling disorientated her instead. She was the one now who craved a forest to wander in alone, a chance to actually miss her cyborg-handsome husband, rather than the imperfect creature he had once been. The creature she missed all the time, it turned out.

There was no understanding girlfriend who could purse her lips in sympathy at the gory details, no therapist who would believe her story to be true beyond allegory. He was covered with black fur like King fucking Kong, was what she really wanted to say. His face looked like a boar trying to do an impression of a gorilla. He had fangs inside his dark swollen mouth and a six inch tusk next to each nostril. He was a foot wider with muscle and two feet taller. He doesn't know I once saw him kill a rabbit in the vegetable patch in France with a single bite to its neck, rip its liver out and eat it like a Cadbury's egg. The night I flew back to the chateau in his helicopter, worried sick out of my mind, there was another sensation building inside me, one I wasn't fully aware of until I found him in the garden unconscious, and suddenly I was sobbing all over him until I didn't know if I was crying over the relief of finding him still breathing, or weeping about something else. Because the tears were changing him. They scalded the fur away, dissolved the tusks like acid. I kissed him on the lips, which shrank and grew pink, and when he opened his eyes he told me his real name was Jean-Louis. He said it's OK, it's still me. And then, when my cried-out face turned blank with the shock of it all, unable even to smile, he spoke again, so quietly that whenever I replay the scene in my head, I don't know if I even heard it right. He said, *I'm sorry.*

As the weeks continued without any hint of sex or sex to come, Bel decided the right moment was something you had to create yourself, and so one night when she slid under the duvet, ignoring the thought that tomorrow was a nursery day for Gallahad, her eldest, meaning she had to be up in six hours, she stole a hand over to her husband's smooth, tanned chest. With a growing confidence that this had to be the right thing at the right time, she let her fingers trail over the small splatter-shaped scar her hottest tears had once etched and slowly down his torso.

'What are you doing?' Jean-Louis asked.

'What does it look like?' Bel's hand found what it was looking for deep under the duvet and started a tentative rhythm. While she was doing this, she tried to recall suggestions from an essay called 'How to Talk a Blue Streak' in *From the Chandeliers – A Guide to Swinging and More*, a 'sexual self-help' book she'd downloaded into her Kindle and read twice from start to finish.

'You're not behaving like a princess.'

'I am. I'm just a very bad princess. I've been so bad, you might have to punish me.'

Jean-Louis jolted upright. His sudden movement threw Bel's hand off course. 'What have you done?' he exclaimed. 'Are we in trouble?'

'Sweetheart, you'll wake the kids! Why do you always have to take everything literally? There's no need to call our lawyer, don't worry. Unless you want her to join in. She has quite a sexy phone voice, *non?*' I'm not so bad at this dirty talk thing, Bel thought.

Jean-Louis gave her a stupefied look that went on too long. Raising his eyebrows, he then lowered himself back into the bed with her and planted his hand between her legs. *Go Sport!* Bel almost said out loud. Next he shifted so he could kneel over her for missionary. He still refused to try positions where they couldn't be face to face, explaining each time in a tone which wasn't unpatronising that mating positions were for animals. In time, thought Bel, who secretly preferred being ridden with her face buried in the pillow so she didn't have to worry about any moans waking the children. Plus she liked the mystery of not being able to see him, the distillation of sensory input (an intriguing theme in a later chapter of *From the Chandeliers*). Even when his face was distorted in the exertions of sex, his features were still distracting – maddening, even – in their symmetry. The very symmetry, she'd read in a scientific journal, that was there to lock her gaze at the biological level, seduce adults and babies alike into thinking you loved them deeply whenever you smiled.

'What would you like me to do right now?' he asked

her as they began to rock at a steady pace together.

'Oh, everything you're doing feels good,' Bel answered. It wasn't a lie, it did feel good mostly, even if his skittish hands seemed to be everywhere at once like they couldn't decide on anything. She just didn't know what might make her feel better. They went at it a while longer, then finally he came, finished and withdrew, tidied up quickly and arranged himself in a spoon beside her. Then she found her courage.

'OK,' she said, meeting his gaze. 'If you really want to know what I would like…'

'Tell me.'

'I'd really, truly like it if you could consider giving up the waxing.'

Jean-Louis snorted. 'You haven't seen me with back and chest hair. I disgust myself.'

'No one else needs to know. I'm not asking you to grow a beard. It's just … well, I liked you hairy. You know – like before.'

'Before what?'

'Before the transformation.' She hated having to use the word, hated the way he dragged it out of her.

'Well, I don't like it. How can you ask me to even consider this? How would you feel if I asked you to gain ten kilos?'

'Maybe you could start just with regrowing your back. That might be easier to get used to because you wouldn't be able to see it so easily. It would mean so much to me, darling.'

Jean-Louis looked away. When he turned his head back to her, his voice was small and tight.

'I already told you the Von Preussens have invited us to their beach house in the Maldives. How would I explain a hairy back and bare torso to them?'

'But the point is, you don't have to explain yourself. It's a holiday. They wouldn't ask anyway. Have you seen how strange *he* looks in swimming shorts? No one says anything.'

Jean-Louis looked even more pained.

'Maybe, if you regrew your back…' Bel tried. 'I could do something for you in return? I know you don't want me to actually gain ten kilos but maybe I could dye my hair or something … new and fun?'

'You're perfect. Don't change a thing.' Jean-Louis let out a groan. 'OK, OK, I promise I'll at least think about the waxing. But don't push it.'

'OK. Night night, darling.'

'Night, sweetheart.'

I'll have to stare at that bare chiselled chest for the rest of my life, thought Bel as she turned over to sleep. Just as she was dropping off, her mobile buzzed like a large grumpy insect. It was Gaenor. *GROUND CONTROL TO IZZY,* the text began in capitals. *When are we going for coffee? Just us OK??! I refuse to talk to Reggie until she apologises like a fucking grown up FFS. Let me know! xxxx*

Sleep would be delayed even further now. Four and a half hours down if she was lucky. Jean-Louis was already breathing regularly but she was wired awake. Why couldn't she congratulate herself for initiating what had been immense progress for them tonight? Was it too much to ask that she feel satisfied that things weren't nearly as bad as she'd feared? Instead she felt like she'd tackled the worst of an overdue tax return, with an ominous bill yet to come. Anxious thoughts blew into her head. She worried at the slightest thing these days. A coffee with her sister. Why did it have to fill her with such dread? On top of the worries about Aurore! Now that anxiety was justified. Gallahad was a dark blonde with wide blue eyes and his father's megawatt smile – features designed to inspire adoration in his doting grandfather and nursery teachers, but Aurore's eyes were a bottomless, menacing black, the irises indistinguishable from the pupils, like a cartoon. She'd been born with extra hair on her head, back and upper lip, and nine months later it stubbornly refused to shed, darkening to the same shade as her eyes. A trip to the doctor had done nothing to relieve Bel, even though Dr Hanley-Davies had assured her that lingering lanugo was common, especially among darker-haired babies. She was advised to do nothing, which only increased her anxiety. Weeks went by and the hair didn't fall out. It thickened. Shaving Aurore for her first birthday party, an unavoidable event in their social circle, was an act of will. She had to pin her writhing daughter down, somehow mentally block the shrieks (basically impossible) and pray not to cut her. Nothing prepared either of them for the stubble. Aurore would rail and cry for hours, scratching herself until she bled. 'What lovely thick hair!' people would coo as they leaned over Aurore's pram. Until they saw the little brute face turn and reveal itself. When they couldn't hide their reactions in time, Bel felt like she'd been punched in the chest.

Jean-Louis repeatedly shrugged the hair off as a phase. It was her face they couldn't bring themselves to discuss. Aurore didn't resemble either of them at all, and Bel knew rumours were starting. *Liked a bit of rough on the side, didn't she? How does a model have a kid like* that? *Do you think it's mixed race? More like mixed*-species, *I'd say.* The girl had the face of a baby bull, a ski-jump snout, the developing slab of a man's determined brow. She teethed early, biting and gnawing at furniture and visitors alike. Nothing was ever enough, no amount of cuddles could soothe her, no toy could survive her chewing intact. After four months of dogged effort, breastfeeding finally became impossible – Aurore literally sucked her mother dry, sometimes until the milk ran pink with bloodstreaks.

'I never thought I'd have children,' Jean-Louis often said out of the blue, as if answering an unspoken question from his wife. 'I love them so much that sometimes I can't take it. I want to squeeze them until they burst.'

The next time they made love it was arguably better, or at least she didn't offend him (as it seemed she did more and more these days, in bed and out of it), but Bel was distracted. In the throes of sex she was already mentally planning the assault course of the next day, the day which had been agreed for her to meet Gaenor. Then, like that, it was morning – the dreaded day was here. She caught a train to New Cross and met her sister in a studenty but oddly overpriced cafe near Goldsmiths College where Gaenor taught English and Comparative Literature. After the usual yabbering on about her students' inability to bother with any reading she set them, Gaenor told Bel she was looking delightfully 'pneumatic' so Bel looked the word up on her phone while her sister went to the loo. She thought the word would be connected with something Victorian such as pneumatic systems in factories, but apparently Aldous Huxley had used it in *Brave New World* to describe the bouncy sensation of sex with the well-rounded Lenina. She hadn't read *Brave New World* but she knew her sister, specialising in the Bloomsbury set, most likely had. Her blood thrummed for a second, then she felt it almost shrink as if boiled and reduced. Was it nausea? The muffin she'd just eaten with her cappuccino was free from wheat, dairy and even sugar, but now she was sure there was something in it, some yeast substitute that was already bloating her. Her high-waisted Prada skirt, such an exciting choice this morning, was now slicing her midriff, giving her a muffin top she was certain she didn't have. But that was how you got fat, wasn't it? You didn't know until you woke up with it, draping you like an ill-chosen lover, taking a second extra to catch up with your body as you shuffled indignantly out of bed. It was the second pregnancy, Bel thought. Of course Aurore would do this to my body. This was not her first attempt, she realised, to prune back the tender hatred that she could not yet admit would last a lifetime.

Gaenor returned from the ladies. Someone had pushed the glass swing entrance door wide open and a blast of cold air rushed in. Bel started swinging her scarf round her neck.

'Leaving already? If you didn't want to see me, would it kill you to hide it?' Gaenor snapped.

'I did want to come. Really.' Bel pushed the words out.

Gaenor sighed. 'OK, whatever. You look cold. I guess it is still cold for May. Sorry, I shouldn't have had a go at you. More tea? Another muffin? It's on me. I'll see what they have left.'

'Thanks, I'll have a raspberry and white choc muffin. The free-of-everything muffin was rather dull, surprise surprise.'

'Go on, you should treat yourself. Want tea with it?'

'Just tap water.'

Her sister rose and made her way to the counter with its wide array of labelled jars of dark reddish-green tea leaves and display cakes.

On me. Another university degree? Sure, that's on me, thought Bel. My sister may or may not know it, but she has just geared everything back to *pneumatic*. If I say I would like another muffin, she'll slip a comment about baby-weight that I'll barely know I heard – a backhanded few words with time-release poison in them. If I refuse the muffin, she'll praise my discipline, say how much she wishes she was like me. But then I don't get to enjoy the bloody muffin. Or she'll just go for the jugular, as she thinks I won't be expecting that. Say how nice I look now I'm not skinny anymore. That skinny never suited me. Even if all my modelling paid for her BA and her MA, and she didn't have to ask because I offered.

A woman's booming voice, unrecognisable but pure in its capacity to embarrass her brought her back to where she was. Then she realised, she did know it – it was her sister, uncaring of the queue or the seated cafe dwellers, a few of whom turned their heads.

'Izzy! Are you sure you don't want another Earl Grey?'

'Oh, OK. With milk, please.'

'What? I can't hear you! Milk? Skimmed or full fat?'

'FULL! FAT!' Bel screamed back.

Gaenor came back with the tray of steaming pots and cups and the sole muffin, slumped herself down, gulped air anxiously like a straining swimmer, and then asked Bel if she could borrow four thousand pounds.

'Sure,' Bel replied. She had her chequebook with her.

'A cheque. So old-fashioned.'

'Yeah, don't know why that was in there. I should clear out my bag more often. Bonanza for whoever steals it.'

Gaenor started listing the reasons, the needs. Rents were up, PhD funding was down. Their landlord wouldn't replace their side gate so Gareth was going to do it himself. It was either fork out for that or finally get home insurance. Waste of money either way, burglaries inching up in Plumstead the way they were these days, not that she expected Bel to know that, she said.

'I'm your sister,' Bel interrupted her. 'I don't care what the money's for.'

She genuinely didn't care, in the sense she had little interest or even a mild repulsion at actually knowing how it would be used, but she could see this was hard for Gaenor. That she still despised Bel for her generosity.

'It goes without saying I'll pay you back. You know I'm good for it.'

'Of course. A direct debit is fine. Like last time. Spread it out over a two year period. You'll barely notice you're paying it back.'

'How lovely to be able not to notice what your money

is up to. I'll have you know it's also for marriage counsel-ling.'

Bel sat up. Now *this* was interesting.

'Things haven't exactly been great in the bedroom.'

'Try having two kids.'

'Funny you should mention that. We were trying again recently. But I'm getting my period like clockwork. I'm thirty in two months, Izzy. I don't know what's wrong with me. The Special Day shagging, the reminders from the fucking fertility app. I hate it all, even though we both want a child. Except now Gareth doesn't even want to jump me. The other day he said the strangest thing.'

'What?'

'He said he wanted me to remove all my pubic hair. You know. Get a Hollywood.'

'What did you say to that?' Bel felt a strangeness in her own Hollywood, encased in thong and designer control-tights. Jean-Louis hadn't asked her for a Hollywood. He hadn't needed to.

'I refused. I said if he wanted a woman who looks like a prepubescent girl below the waist, then he could go on the internet. Which psychologist was it who said "hair is pas-sion"? Bugger, I used to know things like that.' She knew Bel wouldn't know.

'Well, in all honesty, Jean-Louis and I had a dry spell recently,' Bel said. And instantly regretted it.

Gaenor lit up, yet somehow managed to look concerned at the same time. Maybe, thought Bel later, she was con-cerned. 'Oh *honey*. What's going on? He adores you!'

She felt like Aurore, gouging her stubble with tiny de-termined fingers. Or Gal peeing his pants, ignoring the potty even in the presence of his mother. So natural and perfect for the first five seconds.

'You can love a person too much.' Bel said.

'And that's your idea of a problem? Being loved too much?'

'I stare at him and I don't know him.'

'Oh. Well, that's marriage. A lifetime of discovering how alone you never expected you could feel.'

Bel realised she was going to cry, and this couldn't happen in front of Gaenor. She caught hold of her voice and began to speak. If she carried on talking, let herself hear the regularity in her own voice, she wouldn't cry.

'You know, the best times we had together were pre-transformation. Walking for hours, holding hands, reading to each other. He never wants to talk about those times. So we have no shared memories from Montargis, or at least he won't share them with me. He wants to forget he was ever different from how he is now. But – in France – that was when I was falling in love. I mean, I didn't really know I was...''

'You wanted him? Like *that?*'

'I wanted him to be free from his misery. I didn't know what I wanted, really. I was just enjoying being with him. Hanging out, listening to music, reading together. It was bliss. But it's like the real him vanished and now I'm stuck with this man I don't know.'

'So did you?'

Bel dropped her gaze. 'Did I what?'

'Did you fuck him? When he was still a...'

'I can't believe you're asking me that.'

'You did, didn't you?'

'Gaenor, *please.*'

Gaenor grinned her toothy uneven grin. There was something grey on one of her top teeth, near the root, in fact a few of her teeth seemed a bit naked at the root. Bel hoped she would blow some of the money on a dentist. She never wanted to see that grey thing again. 'Man, those yellow fucking tusks,' Gaenor went on. 'I remember the picture you showed me, the one you took when he was asleep. Show me again!'

'I deleted it.' Bel's phone was lying on their table in case

Sandrine the new au pair rang, but she put it in her bag.

'Did you lick his tusks? Did you insert one when he ate you out? God, Is that even possible? Did you kiss his hungry hairy baboon face and suck on that thick black tongue?'

Bel stood up and spoke slowly to her sister. 'You're an asshole, Gaenor. I almost *admire* you because I just don't know how you do it. You always blast through basic human boundaries of respect, whether it's your students or your own family. We're all alike to you, aren't we? Just sitting ducks. This is my life, not your next fucking thesis.'

But Gaenor couldn't stop. 'What was his thing like? Did it have spines like a predator?'

'I can-*not* believe you. You have a personality disorder, you know? Why did I come? Why do I bother? I'm leaving.'

She said this loud enough that her sister got the message, as well as a few other people, reached for her coat and bag but still remained in her chair. My marriage is ending, Bel thought. And my bitch sister and I are the only ones that know it. What would I give for Jean-Louis to have a day with just one thing in it he can't smile at, what would I give for him to make me doubt his love for one moment. There are no spines on any part of his exterior, she almost said out loud. There's no spine inside either. Still, she did not get up. Instead she found herself relaxing, strangely and easily, and she stared through her sister's talking face as Gaenor tried to patch things up. In the end, Gaenor always wore her down. And yet, Bel thought, what the cheque-writing was to her sister, the dispensation of uncalled for truths was to her. Regina was less of a straight-up cow; you could small-talk your way safely across the divide with her, but Gaenor was the one who remembered their mother, the one who dispensed what could have been Bel's own memories to her at will, such as telling her offhandedly last year at their great-aunt's funeral about the final embrace given to one-year-old Bel just before the terrible old world disease, whatever it was, had been misdiagnosed in hospital and had taken their mother away.

With great effort, Bel heaved herself out of the trance and made her eyes refocus on her sister.

'I'm sorry, Izzy Wiz. I really am.' Gaenor was saying now, with something near to regret. 'I should watch what I say, I know. Work in progress, Iz. We're all works in progress. None of us are exempt.'

Bel gave a small *whatever* shrug as she finally put on her coat to leave. Don't talk. Don't cry in front of her. Just get out. Thankfully Gaenor didn't try to hug her goodbye. Bel buckled her coat tight as if it would contain and protect her. By now her anger had washed aside and a sort of grey calm, the seed of a certainty, took over. On the walk back to the station she was surprised to find the gnaw of the little seed wasn't entirely unpleasant.

So Bel went home that day, paid the au pair overtime in order to take a long nap, then made a few hushed calls to find a family lawyer, and within a month filed for divorce, explaining to Jean-Louis that she had married too young and that both of them were still discovering who they were as people and needed to continue their discoveries apart. He refused her a divorce at first but baulked at her suggestion of couples counselling. For the first time he saw how shrewd she could be when it suited her – she had suggested they fix something too obviously broken in a way that she knew he would refuse, much as he was the one who wanted to stay married. She knew it was over when he asked her whether she loved him and she said slowly that she would always hold infinite affection for him in her heart having been through so much with him but her greatest love was for the children. She too sometimes wanted to squeeze them until they burst. On hearing this, Jean-Louis realised it was truly the end and for the first time in his life he boiled with rage and told her he'd never get over it, and they had their first and last blazing row, finding no one to blame in the end except fairytales and curses.

To his, but no other's great surprise, Jean-Louis married one of the single American mommies within a couple of years – the one who had sobbed when Bel spoke of the helicopter landing in her street and moved to California with her. Bel was shocked at the speed of things – the relative ease of the divorce, the re-marrying, the emigrating away from the kids – but, crucially, she realised she wasn't devastated. A few months after he'd left the country, she decided she was ready to date seriously again, complete with official baggage, namely a little boy old enough to put anger into words at his parents for splitting up and a thug-faced, ever more hirsute toddler who was just angry, full stop. At twenty-five she was still one heck of a looker, if not more beautiful now that sadness had reworked her features just a little.

Through Pregnaglow she got a contract for their 'sister pill', Happy Woman Now, and began dating their account man. He was older than Jean-Louis, a divorcee himself whose kids were already teenagers, and his looks were a little worn, and his torso wasn't chiselled, but he had abundant body hair that he would never have thought to wax. He was unselfish and compassionate in ways she now realised Jean-Louis had never been, or could be, and she was able to call him terrible things in bed. If he minded about any of them, he didn't say – in fact, he seemed to like them – and she found she could climax in a variety of positions.

Saul also had a wonderful mother which made up somewhat for Bel's lack of a mother and her troubled kids began calling this woman Grandma without being pressured. They grew to love Saul, too, and when Bel decided to pursue the law degree she had pushed aside for her modelling career, he paid for Aurore's constant dentistry and depilation and boxing lessons, as well as Gallahad's therapist. Eventually, being in no particular hurry, Bel and Saul got married and lived happily ever after, or at least in unregretful and often deeply rewarding companionship.

Only the Visible Can Vanish

You come to London to make it. That's what young women do in countries possessing a world-class financial hub. Of course I wasn't thinking about my part in this phenomenon beyond the economics of my immediate survival, day to day, even hour to hour sometimes, and neither were any of my contemporaries. I did the thing you're not supposed to do. In short, I vanished. Not in the sense that I have left London, or even this world. Physically, I am still very much here, if a little smaller, having lost some weight (a fitting by-product of the vanishing process, simply due to having less money to spend on food, more on which later).

It was 1999 when I arrived. We were starlets, hustlers, setters of scenes to a beat. Sculptors and tweakers of mood and trend. Valiant weeders of the pretentious from the authentic. I came from Devon, and I told everyone I met it was the land of Dairy. I even looked like I was made of milk back then, I was so unblemished. Three hundred quid in cash and a car so clapped out all I could do in the end was sleep in it until I'd scared myself enough to put a deposit on a room. We all had a story like my car story. We hadn't officially proven our status, but in the least egotistical way possible; we knew we must treasure these years as office minions, waiters, unknown actors, unpublished writers, gigging, wordslamming, transmitting electronic music to a dozen darkly-lit faces in a too-large pub. Soon we would be ruined with success.

To vanish, you must be first seen. It took a long time. You might be wondering if I was a well-liked or, once, even slightly famous person. Or what event or personal anguish led me to self-erase? But it's not like that, it really isn't.

You don't always see how something begins but now I can tell you where it began. On the DLR on my way to work one morning, I saw a seat become available at Poplar. I worked for a company in the Docklands that helped other companies move office. Even homely old Space Interactive aspired to be something it was not. The head once called it an interior design outfit but we spent most our time shifting freight and furniture, reconfiguring bad electrics and insurance disputes. By now it was 2002. I'd started as a temp covering for a sick assistant, but she didn't improve in the months to come, and neither did my ability to make money from SpeakerSlam, the poetry and spoken word night I was running at a pub in New Cross. I had planned for it to be a launchpad for my poet and musician friends, as well as my own poetry, but we rarely secured public funding, and the SpeakerSlam zine never went into profit. Within a year Space Interactive was talking about promoting me to office manager, which infuriated me. I wasn't supposed to be good at this job.

A freebie newspaper had been dumped on the empty seat and, in a move that felt out of character, I picked it up. I read about a forty-year-old woman, living in London, who had tackled a devastating depression, not with pills or a therapist, but by removing everything in her life that caused her anxiety. This woman had left her job, ditched her boyfriend, sold her flat, closed all bank and email accounts but one, and got rid of most of her possessions, including her car and her computer. When she needed the Internet she went to a library. She still lived in London in a flatshare, but now her time was devoted to meditation, seeing only a few friends and doing volunteer work. Some of her week was spent on her perpetual job hunt, as she had to convey a certain amount of goodwill to those who doled out her benefits. Yes, she would take a job, she said, if it was easy and part-time, but so far she had not got a job, despite regular interviews. She made it clear she wasn't looking for a job at her former executive level and she wasn't looking for a new boyfriend. She didn't bother with beauty appointments or new clothes. I had expected the woman, named Agnes L in the article to protect her identity, to have a written a memoir or manifesto but there was no book title advertised at the end of the article. It wasn't particularly clear to me why she was being interviewed. Except I missed my stop, so intently was I reading about her. 'Life is often about making the most of a botched operation,' Agnes said. The journalist probed further – what exactly did Agnes do when she did 'nothing'? 'Lie around the house,' she answered. 'Listen to Bach's harpsichord pieces. Hard work and ambition drove me to madness. Depression is not necessarily just an internal journey. It was all external pressures for me, not what my parents did to mess me up, although, yes, they had unrealistic expectations. It felt like my life was full of tumours.'

I didn't think about the article for years. I only remembered it in my mid-thirties, waking up in a man's bed, hungover after a party in his flat the night before, wanting to get up and make a cup of tea in the hope that that would lead to my dressing and leaving, ideally without too much conversation. I had been here before, and knew his kitchen and what was in it. I both wanted to leave and desperately didn't, but I knew nothing could happen without the tea, the tea that I couldn't get up and make. The handsome man snored contentedly on while I tried to do that exercise where you tell yourself not to worry, just stay there and I'll get up, I'll make you a cup of tea and bring it to you, then you can have your tea in the still-warm bed and plot your next move. It had always worked for me and it felt like a self-violation to coax myself, yet still fail to get up. Finally, I managed to sit up in the bed and look around. The man, a painter, was also an occasional market trader for extra cash and his room was full of curios – old coins, perhaps Roman, old paperbacks, piles of newspapers and magazines, a long clothes rack nearly sinking with the weight of ladies' vintage clothes, boxes of bonbon-coloured stilettos spilling out beneath the long gown hems, old-fashioned writing quills and brushes that he probably wanted me or some other woman to imagine he used. Perhaps this chaos caused me to think of Agnes L, perhaps it didn't – but I thought of her story that I'd read so intently all those years ago and, boom, I was up. I felt a diversion signalling itself on my life's road, a drastic detour, except this new road would reveal itself to be the only true road in the end. I barely took in my unceremonious goodbye with the sleepy man, the lip service to non-intentions and friendship to come. I had wanted him, but I had already decided that losing him would be easier if I felt no need for a replacement.

I got home that morning and I wrote a list which I still have, tacked on a pinboard in my room:

Get rid of flat and move into cheaper houseshare.

Shut down SpeakerSlam and website.

Remove all social media and Internet dating presences.

Cancel hair appointment and never cut hair again. Same for eyebrows. And body hair.

Cancel gym membership.

Ask Space Interactive if you can work part-time. If not, quit and start temping.

Delete contact details for anyone who cannot be considered a real friend.

Sort through possessions and discard all non-essentials.

File away theatre script. You don't have to write another word. Ever.

Of course, this great undoing of everything made me temporarily busier than ever. Space Interactive wouldn't compromise on my hours, so I gave up my job and joined a few temping agencies. I moved into a three person flatshare with strangers, and made it clear I didn't want to chat too long over the dishes. I had feared I would gain weight now I wasn't a gym-hamster, but instead the muscle mass decrease made me smaller. Plus I ate less as I didn't have an office to bore me into seeking out croissants and those supposedly 'healthy' bars of fake fruit mulch. My new skinniness frightened me a little, but since I didn't want a man anymore, the only thing that mattered was maintaining basic health.

I told a few friends about the changes I was planning to make. I didn't tell them about shutting down my spoken word night, which, amazingly, had never quite died all these years, or removing myself from the Internet apart from one email account, exactly like Agnes L. You'll have so much space in your life for new adventures, they all said. But that's not why I'm doing it, I wanted to say.

One friend staged an intervention. How she found my new address I still can't work out. See a doctor, she said. This is not the behaviour of a healthy person. You're so thin. Then she said, if you won't see a doctor I'll pay for you to see my telekinetic healer, which just goes to prove the suburban have-it-all working mothers can be the most cuckoo of them all. Bored and curious, I went to the healer, a well-heeled middle-aged woman whose name was

Mercy. Halfway through, she cut the session short. 'Your aura is troubling,' she said. 'How?' I asked. 'It's dark,' she said. 'Opaque. I can't help you.'

It's been over five years since I vanished. Money isn't what I would class as a struggle yet. I temp when I have to. Sometimes I do shifts in the bar down the road. No one recognises me there apart from my flatmates. I spend very little. I don't have a Travelcard, and I'm lucky enough to have been given a bicycle that works. I walk a lot and recognise faces in the main square of Woolwich, where I live now. I suppose I live the kind of localised life I might have lived without moving to London. I'm good at cooking on the cheap. My parents are far away in my little home town, doing whatever it is that preoccupies them. There are a few friends who drop in. They ask me if I'm okay and sometimes it takes a lot to convince them I am. But the thing is, I am okay. I hate repeating I am okay because no one believes me and then I start to doubt it myself. But, really, I am okay.

There's just one detail I can't let slip by. I am pregnant. I had to come to London, but my child will be born already here. We will vanish together in the city into a home of our own, and her father (the scan revealed it's a girl) will visit us and take her away for weekends. I am forty now, the age Agnes L was when she shared her tale, and there could be complications, but it's highly likely I will have this child, which I did not plan for and then could not face discarding and now wholeheartedly want. Then I will be visible all over again, my body a tiny city for a tiny human before I become, to her, a finite animal. I will become a striver all over again before I vanish for the second time as most people do, ever so slowly in those ways they observe in the masses but cannot always apply to their own evaporating selves.

The Eight

Martin was waiting for his date in the Cat & Custard when he saw the Eight in the bar across the street. She was sitting near the window, visible to all, but of course Martin felt certain she was on display for only him.

She didn't have eyes, but Martin felt watched as she slowly turned her upper 'donut' towards the window, pivoting on her tiny waist. Without thinking, he put on his coat and left the Cat & Custard, abandoning his half-drunk pint at the table he'd reserved. His internet date would have every right to hate him but how often did one encounter an Eight in life? He could never have pictured it but now it felt like everything had led up to this collision at some cellular level he could never understand. Incomprehension, he was learning of late, could be deeply pleasurable.

Like a man very different from the man he knew he was, Martin strode into the opposite bar, a drab little chain bar that could have been gaudy and polished, if still a bit unpleasant, but somehow had already faded into the dusty past. The people inside seemed dusty as well as if they had been brought out of storage just as background for this meeting between him and the Eight. They barely paid attention to Martin, which relieved him – it was as if he were carrying out a covert mission they would tolerate quietly. There was a lime and soda with ice on her table (he would learn later that numbers can't hold their liquor), but he couldn't see how she might drink it, at least not at that point.

'Hi,' he said. His voice sounded just right to him in that instant. He sat himself opposite her.

'Hi,' she said. 'I'm the Eight.'

As well as not having eyes, she didn't have lips either (at least not visible ones) but she could talk, just loud enough for him to hear. Her voice reminded him a little of a machine that aids people with speech difficulties, like the voice of Stephen Hawking.

'Yes, I can see you're an Eight.'

'No. I'm *the* Eight. The original Platonic Eight. A single digit Solid. All the other numbers in the world have no substance, as I'm sure you're aware. They all derive from us.'

Again it was so soothingly clear he shouldn't understand any of this. Don't even try. He'd always been better at the soft subjects anyway. Keep the chat coming, he told himself.

'So there must be other Solids, then?'

'Yes. We work together. Or rather, it's like we are knights of a realm. We attend a few meetings each year, say hello, check over a few bills, that sort of thing.'

Martin decided not to ask if the bills were numerical or political. Did the Eight even have money where she came from? How had she paid for her drink? He also decided not to ask about the other Solids. Instead he asked the Eight what she was made of. She went quiet at this, making Martin wonder if he'd got too personal. Talking in general seemed to tire her. She gave him another eyeless stare.

'Words aren't my forte,' she said.

Martin decided to take that as a come-on. He realised by now he was strongly attracted to the Eight. He reached out his right hand and touched her, or rather he touched her 'waist', where her upper and lower donuts joined, where her skin would be if she had it. Instead of skin she had a permeable layer as fine and soft as settled smoke or thick dust. That 'layer' gave way with the pressure of his hand to a more compact, wet substance, yet one he could still pass his hand through if he was really determined. Should he stop? The Eight bent slightly in observation of his hand but said nothing. The deeper his hand went, the colder she felt, cold as sticky ice. He drew back. Her layers, her 'flesh' were a deep indigo mixed of so many colours it had darkened like blue mud. It had what he could only describe as a 'negative glow', a deeply subdued luminescence that was hard to take in. 'I don't want to hurt you,' he said.

'You can't hurt me.'

'You're so cold,' he said. 'Do you feel cold?'

'Sometimes.'

'Now?'

'A little.'

'I live five minutes away,' Martin announced. 'Come home with me.'

The Eight went quiet again. Right now her faceless expression said *confused*, but with it Martin could detect a weary curiosity, an acceptance of the inevitable.

'OK, I'll come home with you,' she said.

Martin would have taken her arm but she didn't have one. It seemed too soon to put an arm around her, even though she had let him touch her.

'I'd love to know what life is like as a number,' he said as they left the bar.

'You are already a number. In fact, you're millions of numbers, said the Eight. But ultimately you're a one. All men are ones.'

As he led her through the backstreet shortcut to his home, she moved at his pace but she didn't do anything like walking. Instead she levitated alongside him, as if on an endless conveyor belt. No one stared at them, no one cocked their head at him to acknowledge he was the guy that had got the Eight. It began to rain but the Eight didn't seem to notice at all, as if it were passing straight through her.

'I really like your flock wallpaper,' she said when they entered the hallway of his flat.

'Oh, thanks, I didn't choose it,' Martin said. 'This place hasn't been decorated since the 70s.'

'I like the patterns,' said the Eight.

Martin offered her some stronger options than her lime and soda. The Eight agreed to a Negroni, and he went into his cupboard of a kitchen and began to fix two.

'Make yourself at home,' he shouted back down the corridor. 'You can sit on the sofa.'

Now she was alone, taking in her surroundings, he felt embarrassed he had no maths-related books on display in his flat. The place was a bedsit really, but there was a sofa and a bed in the main room and by fortunate coincidence everything was tidy this once. He packed the glasses with ice but mixed the drinks strong.

When he returned from the kitchen with the Negronis, he found her still standing in the middle of the room. He sat down on the bed, upright as if he were waiting for a train. The Eight took his cue to sit, taking some time to bend herself into a sitting position, as if she were wearing a very tight dress.

'Oh – is sitting uncomfortable?' Martin asked.

'It's just unnatural for me. Numbers are vertical. Bending is hard.'

'Of course,' said Martin. 'Would you prefer to lie on the bed?' He added hastily that he could take the sofa.

'I can't be horizontal for long,' said the Eight.

'Well,' he joked, 'that would make you an infinity sign.'

'I am already infinite,' the Eight said. She said this as if she had failed to mention she had a US passport or spoke fluent Russian. The word *horizontal* still hung in the air as if she had blown cigarette smoke over Martin. If she were a woman in the human sense, he thought, that could be the starting gun. Blammo. Bazinga. Like, OK, mister you've been all courteous and respectful with your sofa offer, but I don't have much time so let's get the heck on with getting it on.

'Do you and the other numbers, you know, touch each other?' he ventured.

'No. We've never tried that.'

'Right…'

If there had been subtitles of her thoughts as she spoke, they could have read *Why would we ever do that? How did you even think of it?* He was getting antsy now. Visibly, he feared. He'd started on his Negroni while he was making the Eight's and he was drinking it terribly quickly on a nervous, empty stomach. But she hadn't touched hers. Until…

'Martin, can you please pour me my drink?'

'What do you mean?'

'You have to pour it through me.'

She might as well have asked him to pour the drink through a basketball hoop straight on to the emerald velvet of his sofa. The sofa was his, not the landlord's, and it was the one nice bit of furniture he owned.

'Please don't be afraid,' said the Eight.

Martin closed his eyes as he tipped the glass over her upper donut but he didn't hear anything splash on the sofa. Then he opened them wide.

'What the…?' His sofa was untouched – the liquid disappeared into thin air once it had fallen through the Eight. It didn't evaporate, it just went somewhere else that Martin knew he couldn't see or know about. It was hard to look through her donuts anyway – her dark anti-glow made him squint.

'Mmmmm. This drink is pretty strong. You like them strong, don't you?' said the Eight.

How could she know about a drink being strong and never have considered touching the other numbers?

'Where the fuck did that go?' he said, incredulous.

'I had a bit of it, but I'm saving the rest for another time. I like cocktails but the Negroni is a new one for me. I want to savour it.'

'How do you know about alcohol?'

'Numbers are often big drinkers,' the Eight said. High-functioning. Plus we get bored easily.'

'I would have expected weed to be your poison,' Martin said.

'Weed?'

'Never mind, I don't have any. Not this time.' Martin knocked back the rest of his drink, walked over to the sofa and picked the Eight up, balancing most of her upper donut in the crook of his right arm, on his chest. His left arm encircled the lower donut, or at least the top of it. He was a good foot taller than her but she was heavier than he expected. He carried her to the bed, placed her down and laid himself next to her. Then he began stroking different parts of the two donuts. At first, the Eight didn't move. She felt exactly the same all over – thrillingly consistent. Then he encircled his arms round her and then did the same with his legs. He was above her now. Neither of them spoke. It occurred to him that expecting an excited response from her was futile, that any physical affection would be shown another way, if at all. This struck enough fear into him almost to do away with his erection, but it gave way to another desire, the desire to be precise in movement, *numerical* even; he was a number as well, he was maths and she had said so. She wanted that, she had to.

How had he looked at the number 8 before and not thought how perfectly designed for sex it was? Contracting an inside layer of her upper donut as a sort of mouth, the Eight turned out to be a pretty good kisser, even if she didn't have a tongue. His penis was shocked by the cold of the lower donut surrounding it at first; he feared it might freeze or go the way of the Negroni but he knew he ultimately trusted the Eight. If you couldn't trust numbers, what could you trust? And a slight chill in the nether region was a small price to pay for the sensations that were announcing themselves as soon to arrive.

'Give me your millions,' the Eight whispered and Martin felt momentarily faint, but he still gave them to her with one blinder of an orgasm, and like the Negroni, they were gone.

Not long after, the Eight rolled elegantly off the bed, verticalised herself, took a couple of unselfconscious shimmies that seemed to rebalance her, and asked to be shown out. She seemed to be in a rush all of a sudden. Martin slipped on his striped dressing gown, hoping the Eight might appreciate the pattern, but if she observed it she didn't let on. He opened the front door, a blast of cold air washed over them and the Eight let out a relaxed sigh as she faced him to say goodbye.

'Martin, that was neat,' she said. And off she went into the night.

It took him some sleepless hours that night to decide that 'neat' was an especially high compliment coming from a number.

After his encounter with the Eight, Martin was on high alert for signs she might return. Would a numeric code slink into his day-to-day existence, recurring to the point it couldn't be ignored and lead him somewhere? The word 'portal' kept entering his mind and conversations. The vanished millions worried him too. Would he get a knock at the door and find an army of little half-human, half-numeric beings that he had fathered? Mostly his thoughts were the simpler, yearning kind. Would he see her in that bar again? He was certain the bar had played a crucial part. The Cat & Custard remained unchanged as ever, and Martin continued to meet his internet dates there but the bar where he had found the Eight soon got a makeover, rendering it almost unrecognisable. Martin couldn't even place the table where she had sat. There's so much I don't know, he kept thinking to himself at home, standing in the middle of the room exactly where the Eight had stood, sipping yet another Negroni in the hope that the taste would help him reconjure the memory of her in more detail than when she entered his mind during the day. There's so much I don't know. But the sweet void of understanding he had felt on meeting the Eight that strange night rarely returned, and when it did, it was always too fleeting. Still, Martin took comfort in knowing it was not impossible that she might appear again. Logic dictated so. If she does, he thought, I'll be ready.

What Have I To Do With You?

Dermot and I broke up over football. That is what I like to tell people. I can even pinpoint the match that set everything off. Norwich City vs. Man U. The argument took off when Dermot checked the score on his phone in the middle of sex. I always switch my phone off during sex but I'm older than Dermot, who is twenty-nine. I'm thirty-six and I remember unplugging the land-line in my first rented flat before closing my bedroom door and facing a boy. I still find phone jacks a bit sexual. Maybe Dermot's dismay about Norwich losing contributed to his loss of erection. Maybe not. It's too late to ask now.

'He's a bloke, isn't he? Blokes like football,' Jojo says to me. Jojo is my best friend, or at least the closest thing to it. I wasn't a 'best friend' person at school. Girls like best friends. Having them. Maybe football is like that for Dermot, like stepping into a warm bath. Except there is nothing warm about Jojo today. Saying 'blokes like football' isn't the same as saying 'blokes have testicles,' I argue. What Jojo really means, which she goes on to announce, is that your man will always have 'things' that you don't like and vice versa, and that you learn to accept them. Especially if the 'thing' is as big as the sky, so big that everyone likes it apart from you, and a crucial score-kick from a dark handsome man can raise the GDP of whatever poor tropical country he hails from by sheer optimism. She says I haven't been patient enough with Dermot and his 'things'; my knowledge of economics doesn't fool her.

'Even if he spends more time on the 'things' than me?' I interject.

'Better than him copping off with some other girl,' says Jojo. But is it? I am now a bit fascinated by football, the thing that took my baby. Except I'll never know football. I'll never sit in a huge stadium doing a Mexican wave like Billy Crystal and his friend in *When Harry Met Sally* as Billy tells the friend about his wife leaving him. Football is like a town on my commute where I might run into Dermot; a town where I don't know anyone but keep passing through.

Dermot didn't just watch. He played. Perhaps that justifies his love of football to me in some way. He used to play up in the countryside of East Anglia where his parents still live. I didn't meet them as we didn't go out for long. I never will, mostly likely. I mean, of course it's not an immutable law that I won't meet them. It's just very unlikely and it's strange to know that fact, like all the people I would get on with but won't meet who live in Hong Kong, or all the girls I'm not friends with because I didn't get into their school. He told me his father pushed him with the football – pushed hard. Clearly there *was* something to push – he was good at it during school, possibly the best.

My parents never pushed me at anything. They were too

busy writing and putting on plays. Now I'm a theatre-frequenting bankruptcy lawyer and I've helped them buy a flat. Dermot's parents are schoolteachers. Chemistry and geography, I think. I sometimes imagine the conversations we'll never have. I imagine his mother, who I've never seen a picture of, so of course she looks like him in my mind to the point where I almost fancy her – the same pale greyish eyes and reddish-blonde wavy hair. The first thing I said when I met Dermot was 'I want your hair'. He took this as a come on, but it just leapt out of me – I must have spent a fortune in my twenties dyeing my hair to look like that.

I imagine Mr and Mrs McAllister sitting opposite me in their kitchen, while Dermot, their pin-striped, code-writing son, blushes like a teenager, wondering how he came to be with a well-off London girl. Even though he's earning nicely too. Mrs McAllister is probably wondering if I dare discuss babies with him, and might go so far as to feel sorry for me. Mr McAllister is wondering what sort of nick my body is in, possibly for the same reason, possibly not. These days, in the fantasies that persist, even though Dermot is four months gone, they are talking about football and I go quiet (no point mentioning *When Harry Met Sally* to this pair – they've barely seen a movie in decades – this Dermot told me in the real world) and it's, 'you're awful quiet, Cressie,' really hoping I'm OK, do I want tea, knowing I can't be OK because Dermot is leaving me and they already know I'm not the one who will come each year for Christmas and cheer at the edge of the field for their grandson in his first game. Soccer mom. They probably don't know that term either. I don't enjoy the daydream at this point, so I gear the plot towards Dermot taking me away from the dinner table up to his old bedroom where the trophies and the old stud shoes lie strewn, and on the walls are pictures of him and The Team, whoever they are, mud spraying off a slide-kick like a paused TV commercial. His face in the photos is twisted with determination. I ask him about them, joke about seeing the exact facial expression in bed, but he doesn't want to talk, he wants to be seventeen again, hiding with a girl in his room, making so few sounds his parents know exactly what's going on. It's ecstasy.

I end it with a dash for the train, claiming I can't stay the night. He drives me to the station and we text during the journey – he misses me already. I switch trains at London Bridge, so I pass Millwall Stadium going home to South-East London, and think each time how much it resembles a giant paddling pool when you gallop past it. I think this in real life too, but now Millwall is fused with the world of Dermot, a world I don't know and he doesn't know either because I've given him that world in my mind. I always imagine the put down I'll deliver if I see him again and how he'd have to provoke me to say it, which I'm sure he won't, he's a nice guy really, but it's always the same. What have I to do with you?

Baked

'Come round,' she says. 'Johnny's got the kids. I baked.'

It's August. I rarely leave London but now I feel like I'm on holiday, walking to Lucinda's. I could almost sling off my shoes.

'Gina.' She grins at me as she opens the door. 'I started without you.'

'You goofy bitch,' I say. Three kids? You'd never guess. Concave waist, long perfect legs, dark pretty eyes like a bad fairy.

We eat like kings. On the living room sofa, straight from the baking tray, not caring how the fresh brownies steam on a thirty-one degree afternoon. Lucinda strips to her underwear. I do the same. We're really getting baked now. Smoking cigarettes too. Lucinda didn't tell me in words what she'd made when she opened the door. Her eyes did but I knew if I listened I might not cross over. We laugh at each other, at things we can't quite remember that maybe happened or maybe not. Ten years ago. Fifteen. When we were fifteen. Then we laugh at nothing at all.

She jumps up. 'I'm It!' she shrieks and chases me round the room, catching me easily. I am scared, but she hugs me and smears brown buttercream on my face. We fall back on the sofa.

Then – 'Have you ever slept with a woman?' she asks, just like that.

No. I can't think of anything more boring than another woman's vagina, I tell her.

She doesn't laugh. Instead she says: 'You should try it.'

I say nothing. She decides to run a bath. I don't know what to do with myself so I check my blinking phone. Bad move when I'm stoned. 'Come here,' she yells, and I drop the phone with a smash. Her bathroom is falling apart. There's a vintage soap ad poster above the basin, a siren with a dumbshit smile. I already know my mind is saving it for a nightmare. Lucinda starts getting sentimental on me. 'You're the best, Gina. Man, I really fucked up my life… And your face! Your chocolate face! Get in.'

How do you know when you've crossed a line? Is it when you enter the water? Or when you let your oldest friend move your hand to her breast, then past the soapy swell of her belly, down to her very centre? Or when you lie on top of her and her tongue enters your mouth?

'You're so uptight, Gina.'

The bath feels so good it's like molten quicksand. But now I'm worried about my phone. Is it broken? I've stood someone up. I click my fingers, and then the bath cools rapidly, which isn't what my fingers planned. Lucinda pulls herself out. I yearn to want her, like I want to be high right now, not high and bumming out. She goes upstairs and I do something only a lover would do. I make a run for it. I will ring Lucinda. I love her. You're no one if you haven't got friends.

Playing House

They drank too much whenever he came round. Neither of them had an alcohol problem, but she always felt the second, certainly the third bottle of wine was overdoing it. Until the drinking was just part of their routine. He was always the visitor, she the one opening the heavy front door. She was always alone when he came over. He didn't invite her to his home, and she didn't suggest a visit. She had been there only once, the night they'd met at the party he had held with his housemates who were also young guys finishing their medical training. He was still young, too, but he'd come to it later than them. 'I have to work hard,' he told her early on, 'I can't fuck up again,' and her posture had tensed at this, realising he would be the one to decide their time together.

She was between homes when she met him, having sold her flat too quickly. She'd chanced it on the market out of curiosity, but she may as well have been cunning the way things turned out. There had been a bidding war, then a cash buyer in a hurry. Now she was waiting on the two solicitors' correspondence about her new flat, and house-sitting for a friend of a friend, Adrian, who was in Australia. Adrian hadn't been able to meet her before agreeing to let her stay, but he said he trusted their mutual acquaintance; he could tell from reading her emails that she thought things through responsibly enough. A month later, she couldn't imagine writing those same emails, she couldn't identify with having a mind where the right concepts, the right words naturally bubbled up with little or no effort. The gush of money and the now frequent hangovers had fogged it. Gone, too, were the ideas, the intuitions that used to put her name on features and interviews in national magazines. Now her days were underweight, her mornings missing. If someone were to ask her what had dried up first – her assignments or her enthusiasm for them – she wouldn't have been able to say. No one had asked her yet. They were all too excited about her new flat and the money she had made. And her new 'love interest'. Soon she stopped talking about these things. She didn't want to keep explaining how she felt. Or didn't feel. This was a lack of feeling for the first time. Sitting in cafes with her friends she felt an ache of fatigue in her vocal chords just from talking, and her teeth hung heavy in her dry mouth.

Adrian's house had three floors and was close to being a very desirable house, certainly far beyond her financial reach, but even on a hot day, now it was May, the unfinished décor made it appear cold to her. Snooping around one afternoon, she found incense in the sole drawer of the hallway table, and lit several sticks without opening the windows. She wanted a haze to build, a visible atmosphere, but there was too much space for that, and the air above her head seemed to suck the smoke up to the highest point of the house, through the dizzying zigzag of banisters which you could see in the hallway if you looked up. Still, the scent comforted her to a surprising degree – she associated it with her churchgoing early childhood, much as she'd hated Sunday school. Like then, she would breathe the smoke in and tell herself that every in and out breath got her six seconds closer to the end. When her parents divorced and her father told her she didn't have to go to church ever again it had been one of the purest thrills of her life. Off the hook then and off the hook now.

She knew even less about Adrian than he did about her. She wondered what the formidable granite-top kitchen island with its many drawers and hefty wooden chopping block was supposed to say about him, considering how it clashed with the untreated kitchen walls. She felt old for finding something so comforting about the counter's presence, the soothe of someone else's tangible wealth. Whoever lived here seemed to be playing at adulthood. Playing house. Wasn't that all men and women ultimately did together? Elaborate on the games of childhood? What could possibly be real about this, a man and a woman, the man already taken, staying for an indefinite period in someone else's home? Not that he was living here, but he came here two, three nights of the week now, a situation that had evolved without discussion. Adrian had been clear she could have people over, even throw a dinner party if she wanted. But she didn't invite anyone else.

Before staying here she had never had a relationship contained in such a precise environment. It was like they were animals scooped out of the wild into a synthetic habitat for the sake of their perpetuation. *Made for us.* She felt uneasy at how such a simple idea felt so loaded, how greedily she wrung meaning from it. Although she was sometimes alone for days on end, she didn't always feel alone. She felt the house witnessing her.

In the hours he spent naked with her, he displayed the manner of someone who has all the time in the world. He paid such attention to her body, it made her think even more of the shadow times when he wasn't with her, the days that went by without even a text between them. You could be too present with someone. There had been men who might have wanted her more, but only now could she see they had missed so much detail in their having of her, and she had missed so much of theirs too. He observed things about her body that she hadn't even noticed herself, such as the mole near her coccyx. 'Like someone drew a beauty spot', he said. 'Still, you should keep an eye on it.'

He wasn't big but he was strong – in the middle of it, he would sometimes arch over her and instruct her to grip his torso with all four of her limbs and, in what always seemed slow, even though she knew it was fast, he would flip her round. There was always that moment after the switch where her head would come away from his shoulder, her limbs would release, and the two of them would regain eye contact, sometimes through her hair as it fell past her neck to his shoulders, as if they had slotted into an even better place that was waiting for them. He knew she wanted him to do it, but he didn't do it every time. Or did he know? The hours he spent taking in her body in that private oblivion of his that even she wasn't fully invited to share always stunned her, so she forgot to ask him for anything, as she had with other men. She'd never felt so spent afterwards with anyone.

On his third visit he told her. He gave the girl's name. Aphra. She didn't repeat the name to anyone else – she always said 'the girl' when she began talking to her friends about what she should do. Something had to be done. Something was already starting to be done, she just didn't know what it was yet. Had she said 'Aphra' back to him at any point she might have picked another name to confuse with it on purpose, but Aphra was an island of a name. When she googled 'Aphra', the listings were mostly dominated by Aphra Benn, the English Restoration dramatist she remembered vaguely from English A-level. There was no immediate sign of his Aphra online, and she managed to stop herself from scrolling down too far. Aphra sounded isolated, island-like herself. Far away in Bristol, still studying. Except she wasn't studying all the time as she had breast cancer. Had had it. She was recovering now from chemotherapy, had switched her MA to part-time. She had just turned twenty-seven.

'Christ, what are the odds?' she said, shaking her head.

'We broke up before the diagnosis, got back together during her chemo, broke up again at Christmas and then fell back into seeing each other this spring, I guess,' he said.

'So what's happening now?'

He looked tired. And caught, somehow, even though he'd chosen to tell her. He didn't answer.

'Between the two of you, I mean.'

'I honestly don't know,' he said finally. He took a breath. 'I care about her,' he said.

She replayed this scene many times in her mind. She replayed the scene where she asked him to leave and not come back several times as well, the one that never happened. That night she wordlessly gave him permission to come to bed with her and, as he held the entirety of her chest in his hands, she wondered if Aphra had lost a whole breast or even both.

In late June there was a complication with her new home. The council, in what would be her new borough, were being tardy with the flood risk information her solicitor needed. The couple selling it to her were panicking they would lose their own house purchase if hers didn't speed up. Everyone was stressed, sighing, using terms like 'grid-locked sale chain' that made her laugh at the wrong moment. She wasn't stressed about any of it. It was all happening to someone else.

Adrian had extended his trip. She could stay in his house until winter if she needed to, even pay him some rent if he got back before she needed to leave.

Then one morning the stress took its turn with her. He noticed her trying not to shudder as they sat at breakfast. 'What's wrong?' he asked her and refilled her coffee, squeezed her shoulder with his warm hand.

'You were so anxious last night,' he said. 'Your body was tense all over.'

'I'm sorry,' she said. 'It's the flat. It's taking a long time to exchange and everyone's annoyed with everyone else.'

She began to relate the whole story, and then stopped herself. 'I don't want to bore you with this,' she said.

'No, no, I want to hear it all,' he said. So she told him, until she was bored herself, embarrassed in the face of someone who had what she perceived to be real challenges, such as medical exams on which his career depended, and a family who couldn't catch him if he fell.

'It'll be fine,' he said, and he came over to her side of the table and held her, stroked her hair and then her arm. She wanted to ask him how he could possibly know. He knew nothing about buying a home. But it felt so good she didn't.

Then he had to leave, and once he was gone, her anxiety flared with the click of the door. When other men had left her for their own days, or she had left their homes for her own, she had felt full and content. No doubt how he felt whenever he closed the big black door and left her there in the house.

'I have to make another trip to Bristol,' he said one

morning.

She didn't react. Some of the trips he announced, others she knew he didn't.

'You know,' he said, 'It's not just to check on Aphra. I have to go anyway. I did my undergrad there, remember? I'm giving a talk to the students. Actually it's bad timing. It cuts up my week.'

'A talk in July?' she said.

'I know it's odd timing,' he said. 'I'd explain, but I'm late. I'll miss my train.'

She would be the one to end it, she could see that now. If either she or Aphra ended it with him, he was off the hook. Aphra, that bit younger with her health in question, would perpetuate things. Whether or not she knew there was another woman. Or women, she reminded herself.

While he was in Bristol, she decided to start running. The house was five minutes from Hampstead Heath. What an idiot she was for not starting before, given the location and all the free time she had. She'd been a great runner in secondary school – she should have pursued it further. She went to a running shop, had her gait assessed on the treadmill, bought shoes that looked like spaceships and felt like sofas. The first few runs were miserable, but she sensed her old capabilities lying dormant somewhere within her, and she knew she would continue. He didn't notice the muddy trainers for weeks until one day he re-marked that Adrian had small feet for a man.

'Oh, those are mine,' she said. 'I've been running.'

'Since when? You never told me.'

'According to this running app I got, I can now run four kilometres without stopping.'

'We should go together,' he said. 'All this drinking we do. It's not good.'

'We can't go together,' she said. She usually thought about everything she said to him before she said it, but this time she had escaped herself. 'I need to be alone when I run. It's…'

'Oh, you don't have to explain,' he said. 'Exercise can be like that.'

He looked a little crestfallen. He was trying to hide it, but she could see. A small victory for her, an assertion of her privacy. But she didn't want victories over him, even though she so often felt defeated.

He didn't bring up the running anytime soon after that, neither did they cut down their drinking. Sometimes he brought beer to drink, mumbling that it was a lighter choice than wine, but he still worked his way through multiple bottles. He got close to drunk one night and began talking about his first love, way before Aphra. They had been teenagers – he'd met her at sixth-form college. He knew straightaway she was a mess, he said, but there had been other things he couldn't get his head around. She blew hot and cold, she hid truths about herself and alluded to truths that later, he realised, either hadn't existed or had been warped. She had finished it with him and it had been his first real devastation. He hadn't seen her in ten years, not since the last few days of post A-level celebrations. He couldn't be friends with her, he said. Not then and not now.

'One of those,' she said.

'Ambiguity,' he said. 'My first girlfriend embodied the word. Two years on and off together, and by the end I still hardly knew her.'

'Sounds like a painful situation,' she said – the words she'd used when he'd first explained about Aphra. If he noticed the repetition he didn't let on.

'Thing is,' he said, 'I like a bit of ambiguity. Actually, I think people crave it in varying amounts.'

'You sound thirteen years old. Like you've just discovered the word.'

'Ambiguity makes for richer experiences. Doubt prevents

us taking things for granted.'

'Taking something for granted is a kind of love,' she said. 'Trust in a person. Or a situation.'

'Taking anything for granted should never be confused with love.'

Ambiguity makes for richer experiences. It was another drug to him, the man who had once said there wasn't a drug he'd tried and didn't like to some degree.

If he were an addict, she would get out, no questions asked. She did wonder sometimes how much he drank when he wasn't with her. When it came down to it, he could take or leave anything, and that was worse, far worse.

'Let's play hide and seek,' she said one Sunday afternoon. 'This house is perfect for it.'

His face lit up. She'd pressed the button this time and she knew it. The relief. The pleasure in his eyes. She was fun. She was a really fun person. And he knew it. He knew who she was.

'I'll hide,' she said. 'But I'll leave you some clues.'

He put his hands over his eyes but not over his grin. She laughed, then she ran up to the highest reaches of the house. She took off her vest top and left it on the second banister, then left her shorts on the top set of stairs. The house seemed to expand as she gained upward, like that dream she kept having where she was in a house, the same house over and over – one that belonged to her, although she'd never seen it in waking life – and the more doors you opened, the more new doors there were. She'd read in a psychology magazine that when you dreamed of a house, you were really dreaming about yourself. She hid in a wardrobe on the top hallway like the one that led to Narnia. There were even old clothes and coats in it, and one magnificent floor-length oyster-grey fur hanging there just like in the fictional wardrobe, and she slipped into it, down to her underwear now, almost cold, shivering with the anticipation of the growing warmth from the coat and his inevitable delight when he would find her like this. The minutes ticked by and she heard him come close, saying her name, but he didn't open the wardrobe. Why? Did he think it was too obvious a hiding place? Would he open it and find himself disappointed at her choice? She cursed herself. She should have hidden somewhere more obscure, left a less obvious trail. She heard his footsteps retreat, and she waited for him to return and search again, but he didn't.

Finally she came downstairs, picking up the clothes she had scattered as bait. He was lying on the living room sofa, both thumbs keying a message into his phone.

'Oh, there you are,' he said when he saw her. 'Sorry, I didn't realise you'd stay hidden so long, you weirdo. I did look for you, but my mum called and really went off on one. Sorry.'

'I'm cold and dusty,' she said. 'I'm going to take a bath.'

She ran the bath hot and deep, submerged herself and sobbed underwater. If he heard her and asked if the sounds were crying sounds she would just say she was trying to unblock her nose. He didn't knock. She heard the front door shut, and once she was dressed, she found a note on the kitchen table, saying he'd gone to Tesco to get dinner, but it was more than two hours before he returned with it.

Late August. He told her he was going on holiday in a couple of weeks with his dad to Cornwall. His dad had a boat there, a little one that needed some fixing. No internet. Bliss.

'Ten days without you,' he said. It was the longest they'd been apart.

'It's when I move house.' She had finally completed on her flat.

'Shit. I wanted to help you move. I can't wait to see it.'

'I know,' she said. 'I know you wanted to help.'

They wouldn't be friends, she decided. Not online, not in a pub, not anywhere. They only had one friend in common, and that person didn't have to know any of it. Cleanest break in years.

That night in bed he told her all about his family. His parents' divorce and their subsequent divorces with his stepparents. He hadn't even met his father's new girlfriend. 'I just don't have time for it all,' he said. 'And why bother to meet the new bird when it's only a matter of time until he chucks her?'

He had a half-sister he hadn't met. His dad wasn't even in contact with her anymore. 'We've spoken on Facebook and I want to meet her one day,' he said. 'Thing is, it would upset my mum too much. Even after all these years. So I keep putting it off.'

'If you meet your sister,' she said, 'do you have to tell your mum?'

'I don't like secrets.'

She imagined a cafe, far in the future, a young woman sitting at a table, waiting for him, knowing he would be bringing her as he needed her presence in all moments like this one. The girl, barely out of teenage, would bear uncanny resemblance to him and of course it would be joyous.

'Hardly anyone knows about Stephanie,' he said.

'But now I do.'

He kissed her. Then he pulled back to look at her. 'There is nothing I wouldn't tell you,' he said. 'I trust you completely.'

She tried to think about her new home, how she would configure it, move in, pitch some articles or at least get some meetings set up. She had energy again. If she didn't end it with him, he would carry on visiting her – the same relationship transplanted into a different setting. The same relationship with Aphra. It was just a matter of when. If she had any sense, she'd use his absence to her advantage. Ten days was long enough for her to have done some serious thinking, even meet someone else. It would be stupid to contaminate her new flat with memories of him in it. She didn't believe in fresh starts, but here was one staring her in the face. Was he even going to Cornwall? Surely he'd stop by Bristol first and visit Aphra? Did his father know Aphra?

While he was away, she collected her furniture and boxes from storage, things he had never seen, could never imagine she owned. Ten days, she thought over and over. The second night in her new flat she wept a little, telling herself they might run into each other again, but he would never be here, in her home, with her. Ten days. Once they were up, she checked to see when he was back online. Two more days went by. He was definitely back in London, she could see. She couldn't contact him – she mustn't. This time she had to hold out. Perhaps it was over and she wasn't waiting to hear from him, she was waiting for enough days to go by until they would both know it just had to be over. On his fourth day back he messaged her on Facebook, and that night he came round to her new home.

'Wow, it's so big!' he said as soon as he entered. 'Queen of the castle.'

'Something like that,' she said, surveying her sea of half-open cardboard boxes and bubble-wrapped framed pictures. She wondered for the first time if he was a little jealous.

He ordered take out sushi for the two of them, and helped her locate her toolbox to hang the three biggest pictures. He lifted each one to the wall, put the spirit level on top, and she stood back, instructing him to tilt slightly to the left or right.

'You wouldn't take me running on Hampstead Heath but maybe you'll take me for a walk around your new neighbourhood?' he said the next morning. 'I don't know Stratford at all.'

'You sound like a neglected dog.'

'I am just a dog, but I am *your* dog,' he said, and he smiled and tried to bark. Then he threw himself onto her new sofa, on top of her, and burrowed his face into her neck and her hair, pawed at the neck of her T-shirt and barked again.

'OK, I'll walk you,' she said, and they walked past the other blocks of flats identical to hers, to the Olympic Park, then through it past the Velodrome and along the River Lea, and she wanted to take it all in, but she couldn't. All she could think about was when to say the words that would end it. She had promised herself it would be this morning.

They came to a café and he suggested lunch. She sat opposite him and stared, wondering what details she would remember in the years to come. He had near-black hair, slightly curly, and hazel eyes. An old-fashioned face, like a silent film actor. Manly and effeminate all at once. Would she be able to remember this face as clearly as the others? One or two she could barely visualise, and it was nothing to do with the passing years. He smiled at her and held her gaze. How content he seemed, how comfortable.

When they got back she said she needed a nap, she was tired. She had failed at her plan and she wanted him to leave.

'Well, you must still be exhausted from the move,' he said. 'It always takes longer to recover than you think. I'll see you soon. Not mid-week as I have too much on, but next Sunday for sure and maybe Friday if I can fit it in.'

Such confidence. Such trust in things.

Two days later she rang him. She had a *Post-It* with notes

written on it in front her so she would say the right things. He picked up quickly, he sounded nervous. It occurred to her that they never spoke on the phone – he had only called her once or twice for directions to Adrian's house, months ago.

'Let's cut to the chase,' she said, hoping her voice wouldn't buckle.

'OK.'

'We can't continue.'

'Oh. I see.'

'I can't be involved with someone who has a girlfriend. I woke up today and thought, what the hell am I doing?'

'But you knew! You *knew*. I never hid anything from you.'

'I know,' she said, checking her notes. 'It was my choice to get involved, and I've decided it's just not the right situation for me.'

'Fine.'

'I don't regret anything,' she said. 'I mean, I'm glad I met you.'

'I'm glad I met you too.'

'I'm sure we can run into each other, you know, if Ali has a party and have a perfectly pleasant conversation.'

'Yup. Sure.'

They said goodbye, and as soon as she touched the glass of her phone to end the call she began to cry, and then, when she thought the worst of the crying was over, she called her father and cried down the phone to him while he comforted her and told her she'd done the right thing. She decided to unpack her kitchenware. She found the cutlery divider, tried it in the top drawer, and seeing it fit, she divided up the cutlery and placed it inside.

You won't feel this pain forever, she told herself, while she stacked the plates and bowls in the cabinet above the kitchen counter. Calming herself reminded her of when she couldn't sleep as a little girl, and her mother used to sit first by her bedside and then at the bedroom door, before finally tiptoeing into the hallway, deciding she must have fallen asleep. In the morning, it never mattered that she had been so devastated to glimpse her mother slipping away into the hall through pretend-shut eyelids. In the morning, it would hurt that bit less that he was gone, so little she might not even notice. Or perhaps she would, which would hurt as well. Why did comforting herself irritate her so much? The more gone from my life he is, the better it is for me, she told herself. Then she flipped it – the more recovered I feel, she thought, the further away he must be. She called two friends that night and they told her how strong she was, what an example she'd set. If only they could be like her. In a few weeks, they said, she would have unpacked most things in her new home and had some space and she would feel better.

The next day, there was an email from Adrian announcing his return in a month, suggesting she come round for dinner so they could finally meet. And she would go round for dinner, of course she would. Maybe Adrian would have fixed the house up more, and that would make it easier to brave it again. They would smile and clink glasses and she would ask him what had taken him to Australia and back, who the grey fur coat in the old tall wardrobe belonged to, and he would have no idea about her hand gripping the edge of the chair to steady herself, exactly as she had done the first time her sole guest had come round and sat at that same table opposite her, staring at her for a long time, the only time he had seemed to have something at stake, whatever it might be.

The more recovered I feel, she said out loud in her living room, the further away he will be. And sitting down to test the position of her sofa in the room now she had moved it again, she looked at the largest painting he had helped hang and realised there could be nothing right about him being far away from her, nothing at all and at least for today, tomorrow and the day after that would be all there was to know.

Future Digital

M onday. In for nine thirty. 'On time is late,' as Jay likes to say. Leave the flat at eight-fifteen. To achieve this, you get up at seven fifteen. You used to set your alarm clock, but now it's alarm and mobile phone. Salad and fruit for breakfast, pre-chopped and decanted into separate tupperware the night before. ('Expensive tastes! You'll never save for a flat!' – Mother). It may look odd to be munching on oil-doused kale at your desk before ten a.m., but breakfast takes up too much time in the morning, and you can't be late anymore. ('This lateness, Tara. I need it to be a non-issue' – Sue, line manager). You used to meditate in the mornings, you downloaded the voice that guides you through each section of your body and all that but no time anymore since you moved to Zone 4. You used to feel guilty that you stopped meditating, but now you try not to.

You are employed! So lucky, oh so grateful and lucky.

You work in a media empire in the department that puts that empire's content into all possible digital forms on all possible screens. News, news! Breaking everywhere. Breaking in the building before it breaks minutes, or even seconds later on national TV, on a huge screen six feet above your head, the very building you're sitting in, displayed in a speeded up montage right before your eyes, before the camera swoops into the newsroom downstairs. If you're underslept, looking at the montage on the screen for the thousandth time makes you feel a sort of mental carsickness. Dead celebrities, natural disasters, the bodies of destitutes in hot countries, red banners with phantom white letters on screens everywhere.

At parties, you say 'I work at...' and they all go 'Oooh...!' Goodbye to the pay as you go Oyster and pay as you go phone. Goodbye to the freelance print journalism career turned unpaid web journalism career turned office temping career. You always wanted to write fiction anyway. And now you can. Your time is now structured like all the other greats with day jobs. Trollope. T.S. Eliot. William Carlos Williams. You keep meaning to read Williams – poetry will inform your prose too. Read widely, eat widely, socialise widely!

Plug the work laptop in, fire it up, make tea for yourself (and Jay if he's around) while Outlook loads. The laptop seems a little slower each day, like an animal or vehicle, or perhaps you're imagining it. Open Jay's diary, check he hasn't laid any nasty last-minute surprises. Nimble, be nimble. That's the skill, that's the spirit. Don't think about the wasted effort on unused pre-booked meeting rooms and the other assistants clamouring for them, unwanted agenda printouts, cancelled display screen orders for his many presentations that must still be paid for.

So grateful. Perspective, that's the key to it all. Beat the recession, beat the other contender, asked for a less paltry salary, thanks to the helpful spy you know in HR, and you nailed it. The look on your former line manager's face when you asked for more than 25K, a look he tried to conceal too late.

Typically, you've got a hundred unread emails on a Monday morning, but it's not really that much, most are Reply Alls in different threads of conversation. Check them all. You never know where a stand-alone reply might be buried, and once it's in Deleted you'll never have time to find it. Flag the things you can 'action' immediately in red, the things you need to ask Jay about in green. Delete, delete, delete. You can't do everyone's remembering for them, and you mustn't let them become accustomed to expecting it.

Don't forget to open the team inbox, specially set up by Sue, so she can see the team's requests and monitor your workload. Three separate requests for a conference ticket and hotel in Las Vegas. Flights too. There is a discount code for all three tickets to HackMatrix, but the hotels supporting the event on that code are full. This means an out of policy booking for three people! You'll have to find a clever way to justify that when the Head of Future Digital's PA, Rosamund, queries the spend. Nothing gets past Roz. The flights cost nearly a grand each, even in Economy. Invisible public money!

You hear Jay's happy schoolboy laugh arrive before him, echoing down the hall. Japes. Larks. When he arrives at your row of desks, you ask him about his weekend. Turns out he went with his family to their country home in Sussex for the weekend. Not good. Not good at all. This week could well be a car crash.

You were just the Team Assistant when Jay arrived, but you worked hard, and Jay spotted this, asked you to become his Personal Assistant as well. A man like Jay cannot be without an assistant. But there's the Future Digital budget to contend with. They hired Jay to do two jobs in one – Digital Product for Weather & Travel, and Digital Product for News. Before there was a manager for each of the two areas, complete with a PA each. Now the managers have left, the PAs have found other positions within the corp, and it's just you and Jay. Jay argued with the finance people, argued hard for such a nice corporation where people never raise their voice. 'I'm saving you money by doing two jobs,' Jay put it to the big boys. 'So you can and will budget for me to have an assistant and I want Tara.'

It's nice to feel wanted. But these days you are thinking it was just because he'd already got the measure of you, or thought he had. Plus he was too busy to go through the interview process. He'll take the worn-in second-hand car rather than the hot little racer that might go kaput. Except, *let's try it this way*, they said. Tara can continue her TA duties *and* be your PA as well. If it's not feasible, we trust Tara to let us know.

That's your reward for working hard and not letting them know. More work. At least you'll have a strong case for promotion.

In your diary catch-up together, Jay shows you photos of the meadow he recently bought next to his country house. Not just a beautiful field, a savvy investment too. The picture show cuts badly into the allotted diary-rescue time, which will contribute to the unfolding disaster of this week, but you can hardly tell him you don't want to know about his meadow. You're curious anyway. You start actually singing *Don't Fence Me In* – a sort of jolly, demented wave of fatigue and worry has just hit you – but either Jay doesn't get it or pretends not to notice, so you stop after a few lines. Jay took a course in scything last summer. This weekend he scythed the entire meadow. He shows you 'before' and 'after' pictures. The field makes you think of a haircut. You need a haircut. This week? Wait until payday, just to be safe, even if your fringe is out of control.

Wonderful weekend, Jay continues. Nature. Real life. So essential for everyone, especially the kids. Made sure to leave their iPads in London, so they whined half the way there in the car, but the minute they arrived and planted their little feet on the grass – what's an Ipad?

You start to feel a rare blip of calm, as if you are a little bubble finding its way up to somewhere good. Then, the really bad news. This weekend the internet was down in Foxglove Cottage. Bloody BT. Jay managed to get by on his Blackberry until his wife confiscated it. So no email weekend trawl-through. So essential for everyone. Jay and Robyn. Oh, the bird jokes. Meant to be. Jay seems very happy with Robyn. He's very happy with their two boys, Raphael and Hugo, as well.

But no email trawl-through.

Back in the early days, you did want to be promoted. You wanted more money to erase your credit card debts, or put down a deposit to buy a flat. Or both, even. Dream widely!

Dear diary. Jay wants a meeting booked with Julian in Marketing and Voices this week. Urgent but not urgent enough for this week. But even next week is chocka, you point out. Can you cut into Jay's sacrosanct Keep Free hour on Wednesday morning? He doesn't like that. He also doesn't want the meeting in three weeks' time. Can't win.

The building where you work is strange, but strange can be beautiful. Views. It's all about having a view. Views lead to perspective. The eighth floor shows you the entirety of south Regent Street, but the view is blighted by banners. Is it Christmas? you think for the umpteenth time. You look at the church with its needle spike. So beautiful. Man-made nature. Real life.

Back at your desk. Concentrate. Fix meeting with Julian. Who is Julian's PA? Tilly. Oh yes, nice young Tilly. Call her, it's quicker than email tennis. But Tilly won't pick up, even though she must be at her desk – her Lync message presence is green. Is she avoiding you? No, no, of course not. You open a chat window with her and say Hi!
    Nothing.
    If you go to refill your tea, *then* she'll answer, it's practically a law of physics. A tea bag can last a whole morning if you keep refilling.

Boiling water taps broken again at the kitchen point on your floor. Overuse. You go to the next floor up, but the identikit tea station there has the same problem. This site of the corp has only been open four years. Over a decade in the making. Why can't we just get a kettle? you say aloud to no one. You know the answer. Health & Safety. You are Health and Safety Rep for the team.

Still no return chat from Tilly when you return, so you email her, explaining you tried to call and message her. And presto! your phone rings, but it's not Tilly, it's IT calling to say they can't find the missing order you filed two months ago, the one Sue asked you to hunt down. You suspect they don't have records, even though you've admitted to them you were too hasty in deleting the records they sent you. You ignore the feeling that you might have ordered a new Mac and given it to someone who has already left their job without registering its ID number. Perhaps today requires coffee.

As you rummage in your bag for potential coffee change, two people Lync message you at the same time. Jay's boss's PA wants to know where Jay is right now. No one ever knows where Jay is. He is everywhere, he is missing, he is everywhere again. The other is Jagoda in Reception asking if you can pick up someone from your team who has left their ID pass at home. Ben. Ben? You're supposed to know who Ben is. You pass on Jay's personal number to the PA, Margaret, something you rarely do but you'll live with the consequences – it's not your fault he's left his work phone charger at Foxglove Cottage and is on his personal phone today. Just as you leave your desk, Tilly finally answers your Lync, but you decide you haven't seen it in time. Must fetch Ben. You hope it's not obvious you won't be able to recognise him, and that he won't tell Jay. ('How can you not know everyone by now, Tara? I'm trying to run a team here.' – Jay).

You can just picture Jay calling his family a team. My team. You asked one day in a conversational gap what Robyn did for a living. 'Well…' said Jay. 'She used to run a little interior design business – oh it was such fun! – but since the boys arrived, she's given all that up.'

Don't get a coffee. Even if you're tired. You gave up coffee cold turkey after you hit five a day. Now you are too caffeine-sensitive not to get shaken by the comedown on the rare occasion you truly need one at work. They used to cost a pound, now they are one-fifty. Buy fruit instead. Fruit is priceless.

Three hundred unread emails in Jay's inbox when he returns to his desk an hour later from News Steering. You don't have access to his inbox ('What do you mean you don't read his emails? You have to be in the loop!' – Margaret), but you can still see the grim number in its thick black brackets under your own inbox. Ping! 312 unread now. You get the meeting invites for his diary but not all the correspondence about the meetings. People are always forgetting to hit Reply All when Jay copies you in. Don't forward the Group Board meeting invite to Alan unless Alan has answered Jay's query about the third agenda item. Sensitive information!

You sometimes think about Robyn, whom you've never met. Robyn, Robyn. Free from work and queen of her domestic empire. Mrs Robyn Pritchard. Slave to her personal trainer, slave to her beloved children as she shuttles them from after school tutoring to rugby to youth orchestra. 'You have to have tutors these days,' Jay says, with an uncharacteristically heavy heart. 'If you want them to ace the thirteen plus. Or even pass it.' Science and English tutors for both boys = four tutors visiting the house weekly. You've done spots of Eng Lit tutoring yourself in your dole heyday, so you know what these parents will pay.

Alan always forgets to copy you in on his replies to Jay, so you don't know if he's answered Jay's query. You don't know the query either, and if you did, you wouldn't understand it. This used to make you feel stupid. These days you try not to care, but a thought flashes – maybe he didn't copy you in because he doesn't trust you. Oh come on, of course he does. Your general disinterest in Future Digital must surely pass as a knack for discretion. Don't answer Jay's emails to you or you'll just create more for him to read. Be the solution, not part of the problem! If it's urgent, text him. You don't enjoy using your phone for this purpose but, whatever you do, don't get a work phone. Then they've really got you.

Once in a catch up with you, Jay found himself defending his wife for not having a job, even though you had left no opening to suggest he do that. Without intending to, you had laid a silence. Jay doesn't like silences. 'She works harder than me,' he says. 'The boys really take it out of her.'

Sensitive information.

You wonder how you would pay for tutors for the children you have not yet had. It's surprising how anxious this imaginary scenario makes you, how easily you can picture your son or daughter or both of them fretting over essays and equations, holding back tears the way you used to with your own History teacher when she gave you extra time after school.

The emails, the emails. It's the only thing Jay appears to hate about the job. Passing by between his two and three p.m. one-to-ones, he starts talking offhandedly to you about Murray, his old chum in the newsroom who sometimes sits in on Group Board. Apparently he's only twenty emails behind at all times. How does he do it? You actually have the answer from when you covered for his PA, Chloe, during your temping days here. Just go through the emails on your phone during your meetings, you tell Jay. Lucky Chloe, always buoyed up to speed by her obsessive wreck of a boss. That's really what he does? Jay asks. The problem with that approach, you tell Jay, picturing yourself as a wizened courtier to a weary king, is you cannot be fully present in the meetings. How can you listen to what everyone has to say if you're glued to your phone? Split consciousness. But Jay's mobile rings just as you finish the 'ness' of the word 'consciousness' and he turns away, trying not to shake his head when he sees the caller's name.

Everyone wants to work here. Your friends who don't

live in London always want a tour of the office. You show them the blinking, scurrying newsfloor. You take pictures of them next to the plastic models of famous TV characters that the empire gave life to many decades ago. Girl, you are sunbathing in a parking space in Mayfair.

Back the early days of going perm at FD, when you tried to write in the evenings at home, it was slightly damp. Now, a year later, it's a little worse. You're used to it and at the same time, not; you feel embarrassed for yourself, like a houseguest who won't mention it during their stay. This is a stay, it's not forever, even if you have rented this flat for three years. Mrs Krikler won't fix the damp beyond buying you a dehumidifier, which you empty each morning into the watering can for your plants, and let fill all day while you're at work. Open windows are no help in winter. Paint over the stippled black until it comes back, then paint again. It's worse in your flatmates' rooms, and now it's gone beyond the point of mention. It only takes an hour to do the patch of ceiling over your writing desk. You play things over in your mind, you could ask Mrs K if she'll fix the problem at its core, phrase it like you're reporting a threat to the building, doing her a favour, but that would mean serious works, not just tidying up the guttering. Temporary displacement. The rent would go up, of course it would. Not that she'll bother to fix it in the first place, so you abandon these thoughts until the next time you pick them up. The deal, unspoken, between you and Mrs K is that neither of you demand too much from the other. But you keep reading things online about damp. Asthma, headaches, fatigue. Alien spores atrophying the brain.

By four pm, Jay has waded through a third of his electronic residue, while fending off the worst of the ceaseless incoming, much of which he forwards you with four word instructions. *Remind me on this... I've volunteered you to help with... FYI...* Always with the dots. The dots that imply you know what to do, even though Jay knows you can't and shouldn't second-guess; you won't organise a meeting until you've got a full attendee list from him, an idea of length, and whether the meeting needs a room. As always, it's a choice of how least to displease him.

Refill your tea. Drink more, then you'll pee more. If you need to pee, you'll get up and take screen breaks more. Fight the sedentary life.

You can't *volunteer* someone to do something, you want to tell Jay. It's a complete misuse of the word. The Latin root *velle* means 'to want', the wish to do the deed springing up unaided within the person who might actually do it.

Around four-thirty Jay actually passes by his desk again, unmanned most of the day while he was at meetings. Hot-desking is a nightmare, in particular on this floor, but his desk must be kept empty on the offchance he should pass by and spend precious minutes on those emails. Part of your job is to politely fend people away from it. Jay is always talking to someone wherever he goes, in person or on the phone, but this time he turns the beam of his attention on you. 'Wotcha Tara!' You ask him if you can go over some time-prescient diary items, but he's off already to see the Responsive Team in the far corner. Jay knows he must be seen talking to the field workers.

It's not just the damp. It's the wallpaper. Cellulite wallpaper, you call it, that porridge-y stuff with little chips in it. The damp sits on it like scribbled charcoal. If the walls were smooth and the damp a little romantic, like your friend Candice's damp which resembles a botched watercolour in a high-ceilinged old manor house, then maybe you could play the part of the struggling writer sitting beneath it. You tried. You really did. But these days, if you manage to write at all after work, you take your heavy old laptop to the chain cafe five minutes from the office that closes at eight and turfs you out at ten to.

You try not to think that a real writer would write through the damp. Four hour blocks of uninterrupted time. That's what the greats swore by and still do. Impossible at the cafe. Just about achievable in the library on the weekends. But, like fitness, weekends are not enough if you are counting on life-changing improvement.

Tuesday. Ben, whose face you still can't remember after yesterday, has emailed in sick. Why do you never do that? It's not that you'd feel guilty. It's just you'd get even more behind on it all.

Fitness! After twenties, there are those that give up and complain at their slowly melting bodies, and those who get religion. But you won't run in the winter dark. That leaves lunch breaks if you want to hit three or four runs a week. You *are* getting fitter. So grateful for an office with lockers and showers and compulsory lunch hours and a park nearby. Go. Go now.

Except just before you reach your locker, Jay texts you. *Back to back today… Could u pls get me a ham + cheese sandwich, white Americano and yoghurt? Mango flav pls. Tenner under yr keyboard. Don't forget receipt… Ta!*
    He doesn't do this often. He hates to ask. But now you can't go for a run, you can't fit it in before your two o'clock Fire Warden training refresher session. You'll go tomorrow, but that's three days straight where you didn't run. Muscles atrophying!

Don't be so obsessive. Perfectionism is the cousin of depression. But how else will it get done, if not by making it mandatory? All religions are obsessions by nature. You are fitter than you think. Remember – exercise is an antidepressant, even if you're perfectionist about it.

Once, when Jay asked how you were, you said 'bearing up'. He didn't like that. 'Chin up, Tara! We're all stressed. Especially with the Apps Team restructure.' Jay wants you to like your job, understand the jargon, the purpose behind all the meetings. Of course he knows you don't understand and probably never will. But keep your chin up. Downtrodden is what you want to avoid, and not just in the office.

You told your parents last weekend that you didn't want a promotion anymore as it would mean an increased workload and that would further sap your energy to write. You weren't even sure if you meant it – you were trying it out with yourself as well as them. There was a silence. 'I know it's a cliché,' you said, 'but the quickest way to a destination is not necessarily a straight line,' lifting a phrase Jay had used in the management meeting that week. You realise that somehow your father hasn't heard that one before, and is genuinely trying to understand.

Good news, Jay announced two months ago. We're getting a Business Manager in November. I'm interviewing candidates this week, so you'll need to help schedule that. It's going to be great for you, Tara. You won't be all on your tod anymore. It's no good having a line manager in the W4 office that you see once a month, is it? I've been gunning for bloody ages on this. I told the powers that be that it would work far better for you. Plus I benefit too if the department is better run. Win-win!

Gunning for ages *on* this. Jay is always 'on' everything. I've got concerns *on* this. Could you action on this, Tara? You make a point of using 'regarding this' or 'with respect to that' in your email replies to him, which are increasing in number despite your efforts. You don't want little Raphael and Hugo to grow up speaking bad English.

Line manager in same building = more work. More work does not necessarily mean promotion. Promotion does not necessarily mean a decent salary increase. But promotion definitely means more work, and Business Coordinator is just a glorification of what you are doing now. You'll still be Jay's assistant.

Getting a Business Manager is a spiffing idea, you tell Jay.

Your parents declined to ask you that weekend about your destination after all the 'straight line' business. Relief. Disappointment? Relief. Mother has reached her destination in life. Found a job in her twenties where she might meet a man (Father wasn't her boss, but he was at a more senior level, which turned out to be a crucial ingredient for their future harmony), then sign off on marriage and produce offspring. Father's sole wage could just about pay for it all back then. Money all spent on school fees, no foreign holidays until you and Robbie were over ten. Then the good times. And with the good times, some great expectations.

Father never had to be liked, not at work, not at home. But Mother loves him, loves the cold bead of fear he gives her when he wants dinner to be hotter than she has made it. She fusses and frets, reheats it, throws away the microwave-wilted parsley garnish and trims a fresh one from the window box. He gets a piping hot dinner, she gets the relief of pleasing him fully.
    Win-win.

Jay must be liked. He doesn't want to rule by fear. When he started here – they were a ramshackle herd of cats, weren't they? Now they are the ever-expanding face of FD. People have started calling him the Big Boss when he's not around. They didn't call his predecessors anything more than their names.

How to be in charge and universally liked? Another issue you let worry you even though you may never have to contend with it.

When Sue arrived, she was exactly what you expected, as if life were one big exercise in casting. She doesn't walk – she sort of bustles as if one half of her is hurrying along the other. She wears navy linen trouser suits, cream-and-floral scarves and beige faux-leather heels. Jacket and jeans on a Friday.

It turns out not recognising Ben in reception has had consequences. Sue hinted at this. You imagine Ben making a joke about you not recognising him to Jay ('I'm not the prettiest monkey in the zoo, but still!'), Jay mentioning it to Sue in their one-to-one, Jay wondering what else you don't know, don't think about.

I'm not being paid enough to recognise everyone, you say in your head.

When it comes, it's slightly worse than you imagined. Remember this from Jay? *I need you to think ahead, Tara. Anticipate. I throw a lot at you, I know, and I've noticed the correlation between the amount of information I feed you and the amount I get back in return. I know I get a lot back from you. I truly appreciate that. But I need you to work things out without asking twenty questions. You should have a bit more confidence in what you know. You do know who my direct reports are, really. You're a bright girl, I don't need to patronise you by saying 'work it out'.*

You are not being paid enough to think.

Thinking. Does doing a low-skilled office job to survive make you stupid, the way the damp might? Or is the fight to survive a mental enhancer? Your parents worked so hard to send their two children to the right schools. Westminster for your brother. St Paul's Girls' for you. Big brother dabbled in politics (and a few drugs), then knuckled down and passed the bar. Dear jolly brother Robbie – solicitor now with a house in Queens Park (bought in the early Noughties just before the market overheated!) and a wife and toddler. Dear brother and equally jolly, chatty sister-in-law, Louisa, who will always have you round for dinner, send you a birthday present (sometimes just a voucher for Amazon or John Lewis, but always useful – always!), but can never understand.

You are talented. You followed your dream of writing and you made it pay. Feature in the Observer at the age of twenty-five. You sweet-talked all the features editors back then. Well, not all, but enough. You pitched ideas daily. You had a spreadsheet of the ideas and their related red-amber-green status and correspondence, and you wrote several of them up regardless of commission. Then, the recession.

Anticipate.

What is there for Robbie and Louisa to understand if they genuinely wanted to hear it? If you have a dream, follow it. If you don't follow it, you'll regret it. But if you do follow your dream, find a way to pay for your life or you'll drown, and your dreams will drown with you.

Don't blame the recession. You just didn't write the manifesto for your generation or a chick-lit trilogy. This is the era of the trickster, not the grafter. Or so it seems. But consider, do consider again, becoming the thing that you aren't, and writing the things you would never write.

Jay wasn't being entirely accurate about how alone you were before Sue's arrival and he knows it. But he never feels like mentioning Linda, who sat next to you every day for a year and a half. Linda didn't do Sue's job, as the department was a lot smaller three years ago and there was no need for a Sue. Linda was an old-school Executive PA with a boss, Douglas, working alongside Jay and his predecessors. Douglas still wrote letters to people, occasionally notes by hand on personal headed paper, and made her print out all his overnight emails each morning.

Now Douglas is back in the W4 office (a 'lateral move', according to Jay, but you suspect demotion of a sort), and Linda is gone.

Would your parents like you to be more like Robbie? This came up in Session Two of the free six from work. That was a year ago, and you can't afford a private therapist.

Wednesday. Jay has a special request. He knows it's a lot to ask. He needs a two hour workshop, a 'deep dive sanity check' on Friday. It's for a big secret project you know about – a possible collaboration between the corp and a major broadsheet. One of the broadsheets you used to write for a century ago. It will have to be over lunch, as that's the only slot the broadsheet peeps can do – you'll have to get sandwiches and drinks for everyone. Don't forget the vegetarian option! Five internal invitees, five external. You recognise one of the names, a boy who was on work experience back when you were subbing there.

Now little Ollie Bosher is deputising for the Head of On-line this week. It will be impossible to get a room at such short notice, you announce to Jay. I'm just warning you to avoid disappointment. Jay wrinkles his little nose at this. Just work your usual magic, Tara!

Be more like Robbie. It's never admitted, but you still assume it. Your insecurity or your parents' projection?

Why did they work so hard to propel you into the higher state of higher education if you are to fiddle with Jay's diary on Outlook all day long? Why will you work so hard to make more money in order to one day pay for your child's foothold in life so that he or she might fiddle with someone's diary so that 'someone' might make it on time to their country house? Of course one answer is not to have children. Mother has stopped asking you about children.

Most likely your insecurity. But who is responsible for that long-standing insecurity? You're not like Robbie and never will be. But Robbie is like Robbie so everything is OK – sort of.

Linda was a godsend when you were just a temp and didn't know how to use any of the internal IT systems. One page slowly loading after another just to book a cab. Can't I get him an Uber and claim it on expenses? you asked. Jay needs a cab in half an hour. Linda explained everything. So patient. Internal/external. Think internal when you're here. Don't pay for anything with the depart-mental credit card, or you'll have to put it through Rapid Request in a whole other portal than the normal one. Use the correct project cost code in the correct portal. Linda put together a short handwritten bible you still have.

Linda applauded your writing, told you she knew you

were a writer to the bone the day she met you, even though you never showed her a word, and she never mentioned anything she'd seen of yours on the internet. Thank you, Linda, thank you for not asking why I'm doing this job.

Rooms. They all have to be booked via Outlook meeting requests. Set up the meeting, hit the side-tab for the room, wait for the system to load. There aren't enough rooms for the building headcount, according to Central London Ops. The system crashes frequently. Emails fly around the assistants' corp-wide distribution lists. Desperate for a room, will give chocolate in return. Pretty please.

Distracted by the room crisis for the Deep Dive you barely notice as a small miracle resurrects from last week. He's there in front of you again, the pretty man. Couldn't hot-desk upstairs so he's parking himself on your floor for the morning, not three metres away. Blonde with dark-rimmed glasses, playing the nerd but the clothes give him away – he cares a little too much, and therefore looks a little too bespoke. He could be younger than you. But not younger by much – you know he has his own startup out-side of all this. He's here in Future Digital part-time as a contractor, putting bangs and whistles on a news site for teenagers. His name is Ray.

Deep Dive, Deep Dive. You'll have to go external for the room – find a nearby conference suite that allows for lunch, raise a purchase order, complete a booking form, justify it to Sue who will have to justify it to her finance controller. Five hundred pounds of the taxpayer's money!

You've told a friend who used to work here all about Ray, he has imprinted on your consciousness already outside of the office. *Amazeballs. That office is where ugly men go to die,* she laughs.

Friendly, so polite and friendly is Ray. More than the others.

So friendly. But what does it mean?

Last week you had an internet date. You're not yet convinced about internet dating, but three people you know met their spouses that way. Pete, 31, graphic designer, lives in Walthamstow. Runs a political philosophy reading group and spent a chunk of his twenties in Brazil. Not as hot as Ray, but nice enough pictures to make you feel nervous, hopeful. Don't compare!

Enough well-chosen words on his profile and in correspondence to reassure you he has a few brain cells knocking together.

Meet a man, date him, wait for the ring, get the ring, let him pay for your life. You're not supposed to want this anymore, are you, modern lady? But how useful it would be. Tell the feminists it's the lesser of two evils – just a switch from your retro secretary job to retro cooking for your husband, Mother-style. Cooking is a far more rewarding and useful skill – you love to cook when you have the time! And Robyn works harder than Jay, does she not? She saves him the hire of a cook, a cleaner, a nanny and anyone else who contributes to the essential smooth running of domestic affairs. For this, the woman got a degree and shut down her business? you hear your parents exclaim in your head. Maybe the business didn't break even, you reply.

Pete is nearly four years younger. Is that a problem? No, not when you compare him to the single men you know in their forties – renting Italian holiday villas, playing bridge in private members' clubs, apparently uninterested in acquiring a wife or even a girlfriend. Do they even want sex?

Sure. Just not with you. And you not with them, no, of course not.

You talked about your parents again in Session Three. Father isn't the real problem. It's Mother, who loves you more fretfully, who depends on your being happy. Who wants you to do what she did in life *and* thrive creatively and professionally.

Pete emailed the next day to say he wanted a second date. You weren't sure. Just go anyway. Regret-prevention! You replied saying you'd like to, but it would have to be the following week as you were away for the weekend seeing a friend in Dorset (absolutely true). I know Dorset well, Pete volleyed back. Have a great time.

And then nothing in the days that followed. OK, you didn't answer those two lines. But how easily Pete fell away. Discouraged? Did he meet someone else in three days? What does it matter? You cannot find it in your heart to care about someone who doesn't follow through once you've said 'yes'.

Thursday morning. Still no room booked for the Deep Dive. You've trotted out your efforts in front of Jay, asked him if he can find the budget to hire outside space. He says nothing at first, and then helps himself to a couple of your Japanese rice crackers. 'Can't you just wangle something together, Tara? What about the secret rooms in this building? Have you asked Roz for her boss's room?'

No, you haven't. Jay doesn't understand that the request has to come from him, even if it's via you, as Roz would ignore your email otherwise. As it turns out, you do contact Roz this time ('Jay suggested himself that I ask you...') and Roz is quick to reply that there are no free slots. She's even sorry for you – a first.

Of course, you know the real decider of the Pete situation, the thing you have tried to hide from yourself many times. You don't fancy Pete as much as Ray. Does that make you superficial? No, quite the opposite. Unlike many others, you are willing to admit the chemical reactions on which the foundations of lasting devotions are so often pitched.

It's been another full week with no writing done. Not even an hour at the café.

Ray is back in your area again. Is he finding excuses? He says he is trying to catch Jay between meetings. How are you today? He seems to want to know.

You decide to give it to him straight. Be yourself. Depression is a suppression of the self. Find power in vulnerability but first, be truly vulnerable.

'I'm OK,' you say with a shrug.

'Only OK?'

'Yes, only OK today,' you say, looking directly at him.

'Ooh, I'd best not ask,' says Ray, backing away. 'Hope things perk up for you, Tara!' He smiles widely, as if he is always this zany. Slender wide lips that look like a drawing of lips, they are so elegantly defined. And then – poof – he is gone, off to a meeting he nearly forgot about.

Regret-prevention.

Writing, writing. Oh, to be Sue and not have a creative care in the world. To chat about a million nothings, and not have a melancholy that flares up at will like eczema, unresponsive to any help. And brings real eczema with it. Oh, to have a husband with whom to spend all weekend decorating the kitchen in Surrey. Bathroom finally done, now it's the kitchen. Kitchen arrived last Saturday, all of it. They wanted to catch a walk before the sun faded (so sad the clocks have already gone back!), but her husband said if they didn't keep up momentum, they'd never get it done. Fell into bed exhausted. She was a zombie at her desk Monday morning, she said, but she's happy. She got the kitchen done. And she doesn't have to write a fucking novel.

If Linda were here right now, she would have caught your eye, and suppressed a snicker at Sue's ready admission of her husband's death grip on the new kitchen. We'll all be worm food soon enough, she would have joked. Take the bloody walk.

Linda, how I miss you.

One interesting thing about Sue. She is childless. Over forty for sure. She looks like someone's mum. Yet she isn't. Perhaps they found each other too late. Are they trying? IVF? Does he have a problem? Or an ex-wife raising his kids? Or do they not want children? If only you could ask. Not childless. Child*free*. Such freedom allows Sue to work self-imposed long hours and log in on weekends. Jay isn't her boss, but he benefits from those extra hours. He's grateful, so grateful. She's really tightened up the departmental operations.

Sue could use some fashion tips from Linda, you think. A shame they'll never meet. Linda would come into work wearing a pencil skirt with matching jacket and a silk shirt underneath. Heels and lipstick but never too much. A curl of her dyed-black hair expertly twisted up and round in a pin, looping down against one side of her pale forehead. Yet she never looked too old-fashioned. In ten years here, she said, not one man had complimented her on her clothes. Bloody political correctness. Linda knew about things like wine and restaurant waiting lists, knew exactly what to order for the Christmas Team Comms, and Douglas and Jay would always be genuinely impressed, and tell her so. Linda crocheted little hats for the colleagues with new babies, claiming it took no time at all. She sometimes went to Claridges for drinks with her friends on a pair of vouchers. For her fiftieth birthday she went on an archaeological dig in Egypt. She'd done a weekend photography course specially for the trip, and the photos were amazing. Never a mention of a particular man, just men in the plural – relatives, colleagues, famous men and her many wry opinions on them.

Linda would take you out for lunch too. Let's get out of here, she'd say. My treat. Nowhere too expensive but always a lunchtime drink or two. Martinis once. Linda wanted to know everything, and you'd tell her.

Linda was and remains the only person here who took you out for lunch. Quick coffees with Sue. A bottle of champagne from Jay every Christmas without fail. But only lunch with Linda. No one else suggests it, not Jay, not Sue, not even the men here who look at you a little too long. It's not that you want lunch with Jay or Sue. It's that they haven't asked.

First Linda left without goodbye drinks or fanfare of any kind. Then she was gone from any sphere of communication. Well, that didn't have to be a surprise. After what happened, she must have been sick of the place and anyone associated with it, even you. You were colleagues, you weren't weekend friends.

Linda and Douglas, Dougie and Lindy. Sometimes she even had to cc his wife in order to dovetail his work flights with the weekends he had clawed back in court to spend with his teenage kids from his first marriage. Embattled, embittered dinosaur Douglas, doing it all second time around in his fifties with the new wife and set of twins, that was what Linda told you. He'd met the first wife here, and the second too. Douglas was a decade older than Linda, but looked two. Not afraid of being disliked.

Finally a lifesaver drops into your inbox. Someone has cancelled the Big Talk Chamber for Friday. Deep Dive will not be compromised! You tell Jay when he passes by his desk again, but he only gives perfunctory thanks. He is uncharacteristically worried about something. An announcement. Nothing you can help with.

You never saw Linda cry, but she started complaining about Douglas more and more. 'He's a master manipulator,' she would say. 'He might have liked me at first but he sure doesn't now.

'You can't trust anyone in this place. He wants me gone. You should get out and save your own skin, Tara. The job cuts are coming anyway.'

But there was no liking or disliking at all, you wanted to tell her. He doesn't care, so stop caring so much yourself.

Now Douglas has young Gemma as his PA. You've emailed her plenty over the last year, as Douglas and Jay have various coinciding meetings, but you've never met in person. She's big on emoticons. On her email signature photo you can see she is shockingly pretty, as if Douglas has been widowed only to emerge triumphant with a new bride. Someone who uses that many smileys must want everything to be OK, without history or malice. You are generally sparing in your use of them, but particularly with Gemma.

You'd be crazy not to apply for promotion, Sue said in your appraisal two weeks ago. It's tantamount to an order, so you apply.

Friday morning. Ray has forgotten his pass. Reception call you to ask if you can let him in. He could have asked for anyone, but he's asked for you. Fancy meeting you here! you say when you pick him up. Another nervy, zany smile from him. For once, the overburdened lift comes too quickly but thankfully it's empty. Four floors to ride together. 'Thank God it's Friday,' Ray says. 'I'm so tired.' 'Oh, Friday is really "the weekend",' you say breezily. 'And Thursday is "Little Friday".' There is jazz of some sort quietly tinkling in the lift radio, like a soundtrack chosen for your words. Ray smiles, but he doesn't laugh.

In the end, Douglas had no basis on which he could fire Linda. But he could prove she wasn't up to the job anymore, that's how you get rid of someone here, someone who doesn't quite misstep. Didn't keep up with training for her role in Future Digital, that was the official line. Doesn't understand scrum meetings or how to use the right software to transfer dashboard information or any of the essentials Douglas apparently uses or encounters every day.

Linda got a union rep. In one meeting the rep listed her training as approved by Douglas. I never approved it, Douglas shot back, she reports to me but I'm not her line manager. She should have asked for different training, we didn't force her to do any of this stuff on assertiveness training, how to build better relations with colleagues, advanced Word, advanced Outlook.

The new Linda: withdrawn, pinched, dishevelled, hyper on coffee instead of calm on her usual hot-water-and-lemon. She neglected her greying roots, her make-up, she soon neglected her work. It was PowerPoint that finally brought her down. Never cared to help me with my presentations, Douglas stipulated, this time in a password-protected report. Never bothered to actually learn PowerPoint. She could have learned that way before any courses on Digital Product were around for her to ignore. But it's the *content*, Linda railed at her union rep. I could be a Powerpoint expert and not understand a word he says about roadmaps for the new Weather app. I'm not a web developer!

We're not expecting you to be a web developer.

I didn't even *know* that's not the job that's not required, Linda fumed.

All this fed into your own fear of losing the job you don't care about. No one can fire you citing 'lack of enthusiasm', but increasingly you played out catastrophes in your head. You kept imagining a headline: PA given boot for incorrect facial expressions at work.

You went for one last lunch at Pizza Express with Linda, and for once, you didn't have much to say to each other. She went on leave but it wasn't a holiday, just mucking about at home. Then, after fifteen years of service to the corporation, she handed in her notice.

Friday. Noon. You go to check on the Deep Dive and find the Big Talk Chamber is…

Empty.

Your blood goes all cold and electric at once. Wrong day? Wrong hour? Is Jay late? Is he alive? Now you think of it, reception didn't announce anyone from Bosher's office. Except you were distracted, you were trying to straighten out the diary for next week.

You might have missed reception's call.

You should call Jay but you don't dare. The sandwiches lie on their trolley, untouched. Is there time to cancel the coffee and tea order? Think!

After a year of silence, an email came announcing Linda was really truly gone. You only found out because her sister wrote to everyone in Linda's email contacts. 'Linda had so many friends,' the sister wrote, 'it's hard to know who to write to and I don't want to miss anyone out.' Ovarian cancer. Trim, healthy Linda, who always stopped after a few glasses and swam forty lengths three times a week. Would she have been fifty-one or fifty-two when it happened? You caught your breath at the realisation your work email was in her hotmail account. To put it there, she would have clicked New Contact and typed it in – you never knew her hotmail address, never sent any personal emails to it.

Why didn't you write, Linda?

You creep back to your desk, away from the Big Talk Chamber. Then Sue comes up behind you once you are seated. 'Oh Tara, you look quite ashen. He didn't tell you, did he? Oh *Jay*,' she clucks, as if it's Jay she's married to, not her husband.
    'Didn't tell me what?'
    'Well,' says Sue. 'He decided at the last minute to move the Deep Dive to an external location. He's booked one of those FusionThink rooms at the Munroe Space, you know, round the corner. I can't believe he didn't tell you! I suppose when you've got as much to worry about as he has, something has to give, poor chap.'

You didn't go to Linda's funeral. You imagined going and saying 'we worked together', and people saying how nice you came, implying the office to be a place of much cameraderie and media good times, the backdrop to Linda in her career heyday and how much you'd want to say, no, you don't understand, we were in the gulag together and now I am alone.

Anyway, now she doesn't have to worry about Douglas's

diary ever again.

You on the other hand, you have your life and every-thing to worry for.

Grateful, so grateful.

Jay comes bounding back from the Deep Dive in the best of moods. 'Super-productive, Tara! Can't believe I didn't tell you where we went! I've been dreading the return to my desk all afternoon, thinking Tara's going to have my guts for garters! We don't have to pay for those sandwiches you ordered for, do we? My instinct told me that those guys needed a lunch out, and our guys needed a change of scene, and I made a snap decision. You have to wine 'em and dine 'em sometimes.' Then he winks at you.

It's like you can't hear what he's saying, as if he's talking through water. He keeps on justifying it to you, goes on about how the flipcharts and marker pens were ready to go at the Munroe Space, the jazzy atmosphere. What luck that a room was free. Then the kicker. He'll take the hit for lunch, but he paid for the space hire on his own credit card. How to get that past expenses? There isn't even a category for that type of expenditure.

Friday afternoon. Ray has come down to check Jay is OK with him skipping the latest Stakeholder meeting on Monday as he can tie up the loose ends better if he works from home.

'I don't know where Jay is right now,' you say.

'Ah, shame, I'll miss him in that case,' Ray says. He is clicking his fingers, he seems listless. 'Shall I email him?'

'No,' you say, 'if it's urgent, send him a text. I know it's your last day in the office.'

'Gosh, yeah, I suppose it is!' Ray seems keen to forget it's his last day. He doesn't really want to see Jay, and you both know that. It's like he's already left. You want to ask if he's got somewhere to stay in New York. You have friends there. You'd like Ray to know this possibly unexpected fact about you. Your friends could have him round for dinner, learn all about his startup, email you to inform you he obviously has a crush on you, but couldn't do anything about it because of working together and leaving the country. You…

'Tara, are you OK?' Ray waves a hand across your line of vision.

'Just dandy,'' you say.

You don't ask Ray what his plan for accommodation is. He's flying in four days. He can't get into the country without a viable address – he must have a plan.

Weekend, weekend… Waking up not knowing what day it is. Remembering.

They show you when they like you, men. Even the shy ones. But has he not shown this? All the emails that start *Hey!*, that dark engaging glow in his eyes, the smiles, even the goofy ones. The signs, surely? Have you missed any? Don't overthink! But how to work it out without thinking?

Weekends are exhausting. Writing. Dates. Running. Cleaning. By the end of it you sometimes positively wish for Monday.

Except for this weekend. Sunday. Birthday. You're turning thirty-six.

You remember twenty-six, how you left the birthday lunch your parents had made for you and went to weep on their bed at the concept of entering late twenties.

Now you're in a restaurant with friends. Some haven't met, and they are getting on like a house on fire, wondering why you never introduced them before. You wonder as well. Thirty-six is going to be different. You'll go on more internet dates, you'll go running more often, you'll introduce more friends to each other, you'll write more.

When you go to bed that night, you realise Ray never said goodbye. Not in person, not on email. He probably slunk out without saying goodbye to anyone. And you cannot be anyone.

Monday. Sue has already emailed to ask you if Ray's computer is still in lease. Can you give it to someone else to use even though it's low on RAM? Ray has put stickers on it, including one of his company logo. His company is an app which helps kids to learn more words. You could look it up, learn a bit more about him. You decide to see if you remember the name of the app in a few days. You have another internet date tomorrow.

Jay is working from home this morning. Sue has back to back meetings at the W4 office. You are alone. You could go early for a run at lunchtime and they'd never know. Or a swim. Where was it that Linda swam? You could go shopping. Or even grab an hour to write. You can get something done in an hour.

You could call your mother. You will call her. Then you can tick it off the list you wrote for this day: Monday. It is Monday, isn't it? Yes.

The Rats and the Rabbits

Jeremy was exhausted but he couldn't sleep. He disliked hotels, and he particularly disliked this one. Marina had sold it to him as a country idyll, a chance to get out of London, take a walk and enjoy an endless pub lunch together, but as soon as he'd seen the hotel, he'd felt sharp disappointment at how ugly it was. How easily it lent it-self to the bad script he felt himself being written into. The dusty unreached corners, the darkening cream wallpaper. Every folded towel and re-stocked fridge a reminder of someone else's stress. How did we get here? he thought. Marina's work had chosen it, not her, but the place felt almost like a personal slight. She was a strategist for an interior design firm, and her biggest current project, the overhaul of a large chain retailer selling clothes, demand-ed she tour the country. At least this trip had allowed them more time – this day and night was the longest they had spent together. She was the busier one, and she had never given him so much before. Jeremy, a freelance photographer, had postponed a family portrait shoot with less than twenty-four hours' notice to be with her, a married woman who didn't know he knew she was married. At least that was the assumption he was going on. No. She still doesn't know I've found out, he told himself over and over. She might think I've guessed, but it's not the same as confirmation of my *knowing*, not the same at all. What is real between us is what is acknowledged.

As he lay in bed, his mind furrowed through the details with the precision of a distance that had come too soon – he felt as if he were recounting the whole weekend months later to a friend, even though the weekend was not quite over. Picking up the Zipcar so Marina wouldn't have to trek into town and collect him at the Oxford Tube depot where the density of students would make him feel like an overgrown child, struggling to get to her on time, wanting to convey his very real desire for every hour she could give him, spiked with his fear about their situation. His anxiety had jangled the first half of the day to the point where she had asked him twice if he was OK.

Jeremy's photography occasionally showed at small galleries, but mostly he did portraits and weddings, plus a few party shots for magazines or newspapers. He pushed it all enough to make a reasonable income, but found that sometimes he simply preferred to turn work down. So, at forty-four, single and childless, he had free time in a way many of his friends didn't. He knew plenty of them secretly envied his lifestyle. Then one morning in early summer, a physical discomfort came slinking into his chest. He was in good enough health, but it seemed a metaphor for something else, this ache, the king cliché of them all, yet undeniably present in his body. Following a trip to the doctor and a scan that revealed nothing, he soon found himself bursting into inexplicable tears at random, gripped by panic and sorrow.

The first big cry had happened when he found an envelope addressed to him in looped handwriting only to reveal, once he opened it, a press release from his broadband provider. He'd inspected the envelope closely and realised the handwriting was a fine-grained digital print. The tears had switched on like a tap. He told no one, it was too embarrassing, even to him; there seemed no clear reason to cry. He forgot about it until the next time it happened. This second, far greater fit of weeping came during a visit to his great-aunt in her care home, where she sat up majestically in bed, took a deep breath and informed him that being unmarried at his age could start to work against him, both personally and professionally. Then she'd asked very softly if he might be a man who didn't feel anything for women but needed something else. Her misplaced courage undid Jeremy completely. He hadn't made it to the ward toilets, he had sobbed and shaken right in front of her, a woman in her nineties who had never seen him cry. Shocked, she had turned away and a nurse had appeared out of nowhere with a box of tissues.

As he became more able to discuss these outbursts, a few close friends had suggested antidepressants, but this had frightened him, making him certain that the fact of being on antidepressants would officialise it somehow, make him *more* depressed than he already was. So he had resisted, preferring to try psychotherapy before things got desperate. A friend of a friend passed him a phone number discreetly at a dinner party, whispering that Glenn had worked wonders for her. 'How bad does it feel? Bad enough to harm yourself or others?' Glenn had asked on the phone. Jeremy was so surprised he didn't reply. 'The answer is usually no,' Glenn went on. 'But I have to ask.'

On the road, he had decided he would confront Marina

during this trip. Gingerly. He would make it clear that he knew, and that it would be OK – he wasn't going to leave her. He had planned to give her a sign to show he was in command of the situation, that he understood her fears, and that he was no longer afraid. He sent her a text, finally, during the worst of the traffic, once he passed Watlington, explaining he was running late, the traffic was ghastly, but he was dying to see her. *I long for you,* he had written, thumbs skating over the letters on the screen in panic that the cars ahead of him would leap forward while his attention wasn't on the road. The anxiety of watching the road combined with his apprehension of how his text might be received, God, it was nerve-wracking. He had even jumped in his seat when the phone had chimed back two minutes later. *No rush,* she had written. *Could use extra time on report anyway. Thanks for letting me know x.* She was like that sometimes. No frills. He was relieved, but only a little. Had she specifically picked out a small 'x' instead of a capital one? Was there a risk associated with a larger 'X'? A code of texting he was too outdated to know about? He hated that he picked on details like this when it came to Marina. He let her text grate on him for the rest of the journey, and asked himself if she'd even wanted him to come.

No. Of course she had wanted him to come.

During that tense drive he had also thought back to his first ever session with Glenn, when Glenn hadn't yet known about Marina. Jeremy had entered therapy hoping for release, that Glenn would source his misery and extract it for good. When Glenn opened the door, the first thing Jeremy noticed, with some relief, was that he was older than him. It had been hard to assess his age on the phone. Sixty-ish, fit and strong-looking with a full head of short white hair. Faint Mancunian accent. The hallway and stairs leading up to his counselling room had few artworks, but the ones on display were perfunctory and cheerful against the default ivory-white of the walls. There was little else on display to suggest much about Glenn, even in the weeks to come. A Man United scarf draped over the banister once. Psychotherapy books in a hallway bookcase, most of which had long, jargon-crammed titles, plus a few medical dictionaries. An apology once about the faulty gardening equipment blocking the hallway, which was gone by the next session. Jeremy couldn't even tell if anyone else lived in the house. Glenn equated himself with a visit to the dentist. Excavation. Honest advice. He made a joke that, unlike dental visits, Jeremy would get to talk.

'Bad traffic?' Marina asked him as she opened the door of Room 62.

'Completely offensive.'

'I've been up since six with this report. I haven't even had breakfast.'

'Oh. Do you want to go somewhere for breakfast?' Why had he asked that? It was the last thing he had wanted in that moment.

'No. I want to expense the fuck out of some coffee and croissants right here.'

He had laughed at that, found it genuinely funny, but Marina's movements became unnervingly frenetic once he'd walked into the room; she was unable to be still. She started tidying all her papers that were in different piles, then she moved all her clothes around in her suitcase with her back to him. Her two laptops were side by side, slightly facing each other as if in covert conversation. He hadn't known she had two. Probably work and personal like anyone else who had to report to an office and spent a lot of time away from home. She had two smartphones as well; both charging side by side and flashing gently. Doesn't mean a thing, he told himself.

'You don't have to tidy for me.' He wanted her to settle, come to him.

'I know. I can't help it. I'm clearly OCD. But I've finally finished this sodding report. The weekend can begin.' Her voice was a little too loud. Where to put his tall purposeless body in the room? He hadn't wanted to sit on the bed for fear of appearing too suggestive, which was ridiculous as all he had wanted on the drive up was to be naked in some huge meringue of a hotel bed with her. Why couldn't he have just taken her in his arms like all the times before? It was the gaps. The gaps between seeing her made each time feel like they were starting all over again, like seeing a slightly different Marina each time.

Once he sat, Marina joined him instantly, hugging her knees like a child. Their bodies still weren't touching. There was always a stop-start quality to their conversations, which often had him on not entirely unenjoyable tenterhooks, like they were two dancers who couldn't quite sync up but found a sort of kinship in their missteps. This unease was new. Their physical ease at the door had gone as quickly as it had arrived. Before, he had never been able to pinpoint the moment kissing began with her; each time the experience would sneak up on him despite being right in front of him. It had a flow that was always smoother than their conversations. But this morning. Had she felt something was different between them? Room service had knocked with breakfast just when he'd thought he might reach over for her. They ate a few overheated croissants, and then she pointlessly apologised for not showering before he arrived. So she rushed off to wash, leaving him alone in the room with her phones and computers in plain view, screensavers dancing with fluorescent hypnotic patterns. He found himself tempted to check them. He could have reset everything so she'd never know he'd touched them. His hands, dry from the car's unstoppable aircon, wouldn't leave a single print. Others had described that urge to him, described acting on it with their spouses or even their children in plain view. He didn't know it was such an easy thing to fall into wanting.

Her shower seemed to go on forever until finally she came out of the bathroom, smelling of vanilla and something more acrid, like an older woman's perfume, and he had thought *now*, now she'll take off the white hotel bathrobe and it will begin, but unexpectedly she already had underwear on – matchy-matchy expensive gear that excited and disappointed him at the same time. It buoyed her breasts up so perfectly, creating an almost-cleavage that left him wonderstruck for a split second. Yet again he marvelled at how the hard ripples of her breastbone gave way to the smooth fullness of her breasts with an almost discernible division. Frustratingly, she reached straight for her clothes.

'Shall we go for a walk?' she said.

'Yeah, OK.'

If he sounded at all reluctant, she ignored it. 'I know where to go. There's a good path if we cross that boring field you can see out the window.' she said. 'There's a stile that will take us over the fence, and we'll be in real countryside before you know it.'

So she had been here before. Had she brought her husband? Or someone else? His mind spun for a moment.

Once dressed, Marina seemed impatient to leave. 'So you're sure you're up for a real walk, then?'

'Yes – absolutely! Let's go.'

'But you fear intimacy.'

Glenn announced this in one of their early sessions. Jeremy laughed. Until his laughter faded and he realised Glenn was looking at him, but wasn't going to speak until he did.

'I don't – I want it more than anything.'

'Sure, you want it. But something stops you. You get involved – but only so far. No moving in with Alice or Greta despite both of them wanting that after three or four years apiece with you.'

'You don't have to move in with someone to be committed to them. To show love. I mean, if you don't have a family together.' Jeremy found his voice rising.

'Sure. But I'm interested in how that choice, of not moving in together and all that living together might imply or lead to, could apply to my suggestion that you fear intimacy. After the impasse reached with each of them, you saw both women less and less, and eventually the relationships petered out, despite the considerable time invested by all. The other women you've felt what you call "real passion" for have all been unavailable. These are the facts. The question is, what do you make of them?'

'Marguerite wasn't with anyone else.'

Glenn narrowed his eyes. 'As far as you know.'

'She wasn't.'

'Even if she wasn't, she was based in Singapore and she didn't come over to Europe every month like she said she would. "Unavailable" doesn't have to mean another person is involved.'

'In the end she couldn't come over. Her work schedule wouldn't allow it.'

'It's a choice, isn't it? She chose her work over you.'

'So she's supposed to leave her job for me?'

'She was on a highly transferable career track. Accountant for an international insurance firm, right? Three languages? Big Four trained?'

Jeremy blinked and nodded. He wondered how Glenn rattled off all these details. The man had a full caseload and didn't take a single note.

'I'm not saying she should have left Singapore. I'm also not saying you don't deserve that kind of sacrifice. We are not questioning your worth as a person for whom other people may or may not move continents,' Glenn continued. 'This is about your choice of partner. Are these women, any of them, what you, Jeremy, wanted?'

Jeremy wanted to speak but nothing came.

'The point I'm making about Marguerite,' Glenn continued, 'is that she was unavailable to you, and she remained so. In which case, *hasta luego*, Marguerite. But now there's Marina, so we have to ask, "am I repeating myself with Marina? Am I seeking out someone again who chooses their work over me because the loneliness of such an arrangement, despite its considerable anguish is somehow safer for both of us?"'

'Fine,' Jeremy said. 'I get it. I fear intimacy. I seek it out and avoid it simultaneously. Which I know is a contradictory and painful way to live. I'll "own" that.'

He kept adopting Glenn's professional terms, hoping to score points of a sort. The desire to please Glenn was intense. He took a breath and struggled on. 'But it's different with Marina. She's a workaholic, and that is a worry, but she is at least aware of it.'

Glenn gave Jeremy one of his dead reckoning looks. Jeremy still hadn't told him, four sessions in, that Marina was married. He felt duplicitous holding out on his therapist this way, as if he were the one cheating somehow, embodying the very essence of the word. Or perhaps it didn't matter – he often felt he was cheating in the business of solving his problems by coming here at all, even though he was, according to Glenn, 'working hard.' At some point he was sure he would have to just buck up like everyone else, commit to some person or way of being, whatever form that took. He feared the hazy deadline of this apparently self-set task like an impending summer of exams. He still had nightmares every so often about A-level exams, the failure to revise for subjects he held little interest in. Yet often a session with Glenn would wipe him out so much he would arrive home and go straight to bed without dinner, or fall asleep on the sofa trying to finish a bottle of wine. The world of therapy, Glenn's white, chic counselling room with its black leather sofa, ornamental oversize grey stones and huge yucca tree seemed so artfully contrived towards equilibrium and resolution compared to the world outside, full of sex or thoughts of sex with Marina, her daily messages and jokes (the proof he clung to – that she thought of him on the days he wasn't with her), the making do with messy situations. Situations as opposed to what alternative? So many of his friends were marrying, divorcing, birthing away, IVF twins, baby three, four in far from ideal situations, and often much later in life than expected. After years of therapy. Of holding out for the right thing.

'Marina? Oh Marina "owns" what Marina wants.' Glenn said. 'She can work her little heart out if it makes her happy. The question is whether it's what you want.'

Jeremy put his head in his hands. 'I am willing to reconsider the idea of antidepressants,' he said slowly.

He and Marina walked for an hour in the hills of Oxfordshire. The sun eventually blazed through the cloud cover, and Jeremy started to worry about sunburn. He was convinced his hair was starting to thin at the crown and his skull might go pink, even in October. Marina was unconcerned about the surprise rays. She was talking intently about a girlfriend of hers who had married too young. 'She's stuck,' Marina said. 'She's my age, but she's been with her husband for over a decade. Only now she wants a child. She always said they didn't want a family, even though he did all along. So now they're trying. But I know she doesn't want to have a baby with him.'

'Does she know that?'

'She won't admit it to herself. That's the worst part.'

'You could say something. Be the honest friend. You get to my age, you find there are precious few of those around when you need them.'

He didn't want to know about her stuck friend. He'd never met the woman. He wanted her to rib him affectionately for bringing up his age, tell him he looked good for it, or that he was still young, but she persisted with the story.

'She won't hear it from me. Her life needs a good shake, though.'

'Maybe she should get pregnant by someone else. That would be a good shake.' He kicked himself. 'Sorry, that sounds ridiculous.'

Marina stopped walking and looked squarely at him so he stopped too. The strengthening sunlight cut through her thin shirt, glowing white through her unfastened jacket, revealing the contours of the satin bra in a way that was impossible to ignore. He trained his eyes firmly to meet her now slightly accusatory ones in that moment. 'I never expected you to say that sort of thing,' she said.

'Sorry,' Jeremy said. 'I'm thinking aloud. It's just that I've seen it happen to the most unlikely people. At the risk of sounding naive, I have noticed that once in a while these mad situations work out for the best.' God, I never know what to say with you, he thought.

'I don't think that sort of thing ever does.' Marina replied.

After they finished their walk, it was problematic finding somewhere to eat. The place Marina had in mind, a pub that looked like a country manor, standing alone on the quiet road they had reached, was closed for a wedding reception. Jeremy wanted to Google some other options, but his phone couldn't even get a signal. Marina got a recommendation from the pub owner, they then got lost trying to find The Novice; her phone was able to get a map, but then the battery died. Every setback plunged him into fear laced with an additional anxiety at the flux of his own emotions. He hated feeling like this, but he managed to hide it. Mostly. He felt Marina observing this side of him, this chewed-up person that was him, and also very much a distortion of him. He sensed a warm, quiet tolerance from her, which he worried was indifference. Finally they were seated, ordering food at The Novice, the kind of rustic or faux-rustic place Jeremy had imagined they'd have lunch at, the many times he'd imagined this day. As soon as he was opposite her, face to face, breaking up pieces of warm bread, he felt instantly better. It felt so strange to picture a fantasy, and then for it to become a physical reality so close to what he had pictured.

After lunch there was more walking – she was determined to discover a different route back to the hotel, and finally at the kissing gate at the end of one field they kissed, giggling as if it were the law, and Marina took his hand and held it for the rest of the walk back, her thumb stroking his with tiny shy movements, eyes darting back and forth as they walked side by side.

Once they were back in her hotel room, there was the real ease he wanted, that he'd feared they'd lost. They started to take their clothes off mid-conversation. Each action seemed to be a physical extension of whatever they were talking about. Jeremy could hardly remember that conversation when he tried to replay it in his mind, (even the next day). It was the having it, the having of each other that mattered above the words and they knew that. Which made it even better.

'This is the second time you've mentioned the rabbits.' Glenn said. It was their fifth session or maybe their sixth.

Jeremy shrugged. He hadn't noticed. He had noticed, however, that since his second week on Citalopram he had been having some bizarre dreams. He also had a constantly dry mouth, which meant he had to chew gum to salivate properly. At home he sucked ice cubes. He had been terrified of erectile dysfunction, but so far it hadn't been a problem. But the dreams! He'd never had such dreams in his life. Often they were trippy rehashes of details that came unstuck from daily life, but the rabbit dream was clear as day and it kept coming back.

'I read this article,' Jeremy said. 'It spooked me. I keep thinking about it.'

He told Glenn about Canna, an island twenty-three miles off the northwest coast of Scotland. It had only a dozen residents. Something like sixteen thousand rabbits lived there, burrowing the island to the point where they were causing landslides and exposing graves. Entire buildings were collapsing, and one landslide had blocked a whole road. The sea eagles had fed on the rabbits, but now they hardly made a dent in their population. What fascinated Jeremy was that only seven years earlier, the island had had a rat infestation. It had cost over half a million pounds to eradicate ten thousand rats. Now the island was worse off, as the rat removal had led to the rabbit population booming out of control. There was a futility to the story, the sweeping away of animals like water on a windscreen, that Jeremy found irresistible.

After they finished having sex, he and Marina lay side by side on their backs, staring upwards. He wondered what sort of picture they made together, like this. He remembered stroking her left arm, the skin so soft it seemed almost liquid in its pliability. They were silent as he did this, and for the first time that day Jeremy felt he could truly relax, that the warmth of this shared silence was an achievement between them. Then Marina spoke.

'I've got something to tell you.'

'Oh?'

'Earlier today, when you said that my friend should consider having a baby out of wedlock.'

'Oh, yes.'

'God, "out of wedlock". It sounds so medieval doesn't it? I don't know why I picked those words. Anyway, I think I reacted badly to what you said.'

This is it, Jeremy told himself, bracing.

'I shouldn't have talked that way about someone I don't know,' he said. 'Or even if I did know her, it's not a helpful thing to say.'

'No, no, I was worried I may have seemed angry or cold when we were talking about it. It's just…'

They turned on their sides to face each other.

'Go on,' he said.

'It applies to me,' Marina said.

Now, Jeremy told himself. Now. She is on the bridge, reaching for you. Meet her on the bridge and get her across before it collapses. Tell her you know. Tell her everything will be OK.

He couldn't speak. For the life of him, he couldn't.

'My mother died two years ago,' Marina went on. 'A few days after the funeral, my sister Rachel and I went to help my aunt go through my mum's things, and she sat us down and told us that our parents weren't our real parents.'

'What?'

'I don't know why my mother never told us.'

'That's a huge, crazy thing not to tell.'

'I think she was planning to. But our dad died when we were ten – we're twins – from a heart attack; she was devastated, and just left it later and later until it became too strange and big for her to tell. Then she died.'

'So who are your real parents?'

'All I found out from my aunt is our biological mother got pregnant by someone when she was on holiday in Sweden, and couldn't raise twins alone. She tried for six months and she couldn't cope so she gave us up for adoption. We were pretty lucky. Our adoptive mother – Mum – she had everything. Husband, big house, a whole clan ready to help, plenty of money. She just couldn't have kids.'

'What a situation to find yourself in. I can't imagine.'

'It's pretty bonkers. Bet you weren't expecting that.'

'Actually, I thought you were going to tell me something quite different,' Jeremy said.

'Well,' said Marina. 'I just wanted to explain why I was getting a bit queasy when we were talking about my friend earlier. She's so unhappy, and it really gets to me. I want to speak up and help her. But I just don't have the strength when the moment arrives. If it would even make a difference.'

Jeremy reached over for her and wrapped his leg over her thighs. They kissed. He began to stroke her hair, and then his hands ran over the rest of her body. Marina made some excited murmurs, but then pulled back and met his eyes.

'Jeremy.'

'Yes?'

'Thanks for understanding. Thanks for being so nice. I feel I can trust you, and that I could tell you anything.'

They had sex again and went downstairs to eat before the kitchen closed. The food wasn't great, an overcooked steak with damp chips, but he was so horny he barely registered it. He could hardly eat anyway. All he wanted was to have sex with her again after the meal but she fell asleep as he was brushing his teeth. He remembered she was tired from getting up so early and decided not to wake her.

How easily she curved her body to his in the night, eyes remaining shut. Did she do that with her husband? Did she ever worry about saying his name in bed with Jeremy? Or the other way round? Wondering about her calling out the wrong name in her sleep was up there with the 'heartache' that had sent him to the doctor. Heartache. A hotel room with a married woman whom he had, so far, chosen not to confront, but now he could see it wasn't a choice but a failure of will marauding as patience.

Dead parents who had never been her biological parents. He found it laughable that he was having these thoughts about these very things at three in the morning. Before he'd met Marina he hadn't had to consider such things. With the other women he had always felt like he was waiting for everything to take on its own momentum, for the world and its events to really happen. With her he felt something like perpetual motion sickness. Then, fuck her, he thought. She'll wake in the night and she'll just go back to sleep. I will lie next to her wondering what the hell to say in the morning before she has to rush off to her friend's wedding in Leeds. Where she will meet her husband.

He gently removed her arm from his ribs and eased himself out of the bed, which gave a creak. It didn't wake her. He didn't even bother to close the bathroom door properly as he filled a glass with tap water and gulped it down, then another. *I trust you and I could tell you anything. Thanks for being so nice.* Fuck her and fuck her husband. The cuckold. That was the kind of word Marina would probably use. Wedlock. Cuckold. She liked these olde worlde terms, and he had to admit, every time she used one he felt his cock go limp, his brain squirm. She didn't know how pretentious she sounded, clearly one of those 'English is such a rich language and we don't use enough of it' beat you at Scrabble literary wannabes. Doubt seeped its way through him as he sat on the edge of the bathtub. He had to confront her this morning, he couldn't face himself otherwise. In less than seven hours he and Marina would be in their separate cars driving in opposite directions across England.

He heard a noise in the bedroom, a rustling. Was she awake? Was she coming to the bathroom? He found himself on edge as if there was something behind the half-open door to be genuinely afraid of. Then his mind switched back to the fix he was in. Clearly he would appear to have been thinking, distancing himself from her. How to explain? I can't sleep. Why can't you sleep? I just can't, he would say. One of those nights.

The rustling. There it was again. He was amazed it hadn't disturbed her. Apart from that noise it was so quiet in the room, so lacking in city sounds he was now able to hear her hushed breathing in the bed, the deep silent pauses she took between breaths as if she might never breathe again and yet, as always, the breath began again just when you thought how unusual, how utterly *definitive* it would be if it just stopped. She said her mother had died in the night, gone to bed with supposed flu, which turned out to be meningitis. She was found dead two days later by a neighbour who had lent her his toolkit and, urgently needing it back, let himself in after seeing a light on but getting no response from the house. Again, that rustling. If it wasn't Marina, it had to be an animal. The size of the sounds dictated it was probably a rat. In bed, they had scoffed some biscuits they'd found in little packets on the dresser opposite the bed. He'd thrown away a half-eaten one. Now a rat, sniffing it out, might have fallen in the bin. It had probably flipped the lid shut with its movements and now couldn't get out. But how would it have shimmied up the slippery vertical metal? His weary mind couldn't make sense of it. He wandered slowly back to bed, and even though he knew he should have freed the rat, real or imaginary but probably real, no doubt gnawing its way into deepest madness, he ignored it, not wanting to admit to himself that he was afraid to look. Now, in the bed staring at Marina again, he felt too wired to sleep.

'So you never asked her,' Glenn said.

No, Jeremy hadn't asked if Marina was with anyone when he'd met her. And not after, either. But he had, arguably, checked when he met her. It was the kind of checking he didn't always know he was doing, but he had gone down all the usual channels. Listened out for signs of a live-in partner or flatmates, (people had flatmates at all sorts of life stages now, even if they were earning good money, didn't they?), listened for the 'we' that never came, and he'd drawn the conclusion that she was just another well-heeled thirtysomething career woman who probably lived alone. She wasn't on Facebook or Twitter, but she was on Linked In, and nothing was mentioned there about her marriage. So he'd assumed she was single or single enough. She was clearly a catch, but parties, when people still bothered to have them, were teeming with these alluring, carefully-put-together older 'girls', out there making the effort, and the men in attendance were either married or perpetually unattached. No wonder Marina had bounded up to him. They had talked for a long time and exchanged business cards. He'd fancied her straight away. After that, a week had gone by without contact. Jeremy was busy, or thought he was. He had thought about calling her, texting, but the thoughts didn't latch together enough to justify action. In the end it hadn't mattered, as Marina had called him. Practically invited herself over. The unrecognisable flashing number, her voice on the phone, it was a complete thrill, too simple and good to be true.

The discovery of her marriage hadn't been dramatic. A month into their affair, he had Googled her. Finding very little apart from her listing in the company she'd worked for and a few photographs of her at some slightly aristocratic countryside party, he had Googled just her surname. Beecraft. A man had appeared with a blog. Howard Beecraft. Medieval fonts. That was Howard Beecraft's thing. Instantly bored, Jeremy had nearly closed the page until: 'Marina still finds my hobby laughable...' the second most recent entry began. Sister? There wasn't a photo of Howard anywhere online. He read on until he had felt a sort of nauseous fizzing around his eyes and nose, an unpleasant rising of his chest when he'd found what he'd been snooping for. *My wife, Marina, prefers to spend her free time…* Did she want to be caught out? Or did they have some sort of open arrangement? If so, why hadn't she said so? Was she afraid she'd lose him? Or lose Howard? Was the market for bits on the side for married women lacking in recruits? Was theirs a marriage that needed the force of a crisis to drive it to its anticipated end? Then it occurred to him that she might not know about the blog, 'laughable' implying she was not a follower or participant in the world of old English script. He had asked himself if he'd been a weirdo for Googling her. If he argued to himself that he was within his rights to use the internet to discover unsavoury facts about a woman he was seeing for his own self-preservation, well, that wasn't a world he wanted to live in.

Straightaway, before he lost his nerve, before he mentally reconfigured every sign she may or not have given him that she was indeed married ('plus you had the green light you needed – proof she wasn't available,' Glenn remarked) he had rung Marina with the intention of fixing things face to face. Like an adult. Explain he couldn't be involved with someone married. Set an example. She couldn't get away with it ('Why *bother* to meet her in person to end it?' Glenn asked. 'Why not just a phone call? She has hardly been precious in her dealings with you.'). In the end all he'd managed to say was that he had to see her. Tomorrow. He'd booked a restaurant. Quite reasonably, she had mistaken his urgency for extra ardour. Then, when he saw her, dressed up for the classy restaurant she'd suggested, blatantly confident in her ability to fire him up, the ardour showed up for real, delaying the confrontation that had seemed so inevitable on entering the restaurant.

It seemed to him that he believed every last opinion of his ever-changing mind, like a hanging juror. Which rendered his opinions useless.

He met Glenn's eyes, and found himself welling up again. Neither of them spoke for a moment. Glenn handed him a box of tissues.

'To ask if someone is taken is to risk the pain of getting an answer you don't want,' Glenn said.

Jeremy nodded in agreement.

'But what you do with that answer is your decision. You are an adult free to choose your best actions with the information you have. Asking someone if they are married is perhaps unromantic. It's also a perfectly reasonable question for one adult to ask another. In small-talk contexts, even.'

Jeremy had almost asked Glenn if he was married then and there out of spite. Then he saw Glenn wore a plain gold wedding ring. Why hadn't he noticed it before?

'I can't take it,' Jeremy said. 'I don't know if I can do this again.'

He saw a flash of concern over Glenn's face.

'What's the thing you can't take, Jeremy? What are the tears about?'

'I don't know. Really. I don't.' Jeremy began to sob.

There was a silence before Glenn spoke again.

'I know this is hard. But when you lose, don't lose the lesson. When you next find yourself interested in someone, you ask Marina or Marguerite or whoever, "Are you married?" and she says "yes" and you say "Tell me about your husband." Or perhaps you don't. Perhaps it's "how dare you not tell me" before kissing me, inviting me round, or whatever it is. At which point she says oh, I'm sorry, I guess it's over if you don't want it this way. Or I like you but I can only offer you weekends. At which point you say "thanks but no thanks" and walk away.'

'You make it sound so simple,' Jeremy said.

'Love is so often about saying no. No, I won't put up with this. No, I didn't like that when you said that yesterday. Imagine you have a toolkit. Everyone has a toolkit. Which tools do you get out for which occasion? Asking brings good news either way. Either she's taken and you bin her or she's not and you pursue things further.'

He thought about Glenn that night in the hotel room. Had Glenn ever had to rip himself away from someone? He considered his options if he didn't break up with Marina this very morning. A phone call? A meeting? How did you break up with someone else's wife who could only see you with ever decreasing regularity? Was that worth a Google? He pictured destroying the prints he'd kept of some pictures he'd taken of her, and was surprised at how appealing it seemed. He'd erase the files of her on the computer as well. Get rid of her number. Delete the entire thread of their text messages. Thank goodness she wasn't on Facebook. But the sodding internet. He couldn't remove her from his website. The series of portraits he'd done of her was one of his best ever. Had she shown his website to Howard? Did Howard feel a trace of jealousy that another man had captured his wife so well on camera, or did he not give a fuck? He'd try not to think about her, try not to search for her online ever again, try not let the portrait on his website fill the screen with her face, but he knew the mere effort of suppression would hurt in a whole other way – as it had done with Marguerite, who now hardly crossed his mind.

It sometimes saddened him that he barely thought about Marguerite, even though he'd discussed her with Glenn, even though she had been the last one before Marina. Would it be that way again? If it's over, I'll have a few bad weeks, he thought. The first month is always the worst. Or was it? For him the first month of a break up was always adrenaline-fuelled by incredulity and the possibility of reunion. Friends would cluster round, baby him like he had a bad cold. It was the second and third months that hit harder – when he'd be old gossip, when a memory would erupt less frequently, but it became a hyperreal scene from the now extinguished movie of your life, a vision that could knock you sideways for an evening, or sour a whole day's work.

He imagined not knowing Marina anymore, running into her in six months, years, decades even. He began toying with the idea of the need to be on his guard for the inevitable collision, the one that had to happen, had always happened with the others. She'd be divorced by then. He would have finished his 'process' with Glenn. Soon he wouldn't be able to keep up the expense of therapy anyway. The other loves were mostly out of his life, save the occasional coffee or chance appearance at his photography exhibitions. The exhibitions were useful in the opportunity they gave to recreate the entire population of his life, maintain a kind of perennial contact that sometimes took the edge off the grief of losing a love. He always invited Marguerite as a kind of dark joke between them, this whimsy they shared that she might be passing through London. He wouldn't be inviting Marina if it was over. He already knew that.

He drifted eventually off to sleep with these thoughts and dreamt he was holding a woman's hand. A woman that was not quite Marina but another of the occasional mystery women he would meet in dreams. He didn't know how he dreamt up whole people he had never met but he did it now more than ever. Whenever he woke he couldn't believe they weren't real, identifiable women. Some of these women were and weren't Marina all at once, like the way she seemed a little different each time he saw her. He conjured up whole scenarios with her in his waking life, sometimes getting close to speaking out loud to her when she wasn't there, playing her a song, retelling an anecdote from a friend that pertained specially to her. Sometimes he would text or email her with these thoughts, but he didn't allow himself this pleasure too often, as there was always the fear she wouldn't answer him, that at any moment she would pull the plug, having someone to grasp onto. He woke up and realised his fingers were partially interlaced with hers. The interlaced hand had an itch near the wrist, he could have sworn it was an October-resistant mosquito, but he didn't want to let go of her hand and the slight clasp it was exercising, even though she remained in her deep sleep. He wondered if she had taken a pill to sleep, a thought that filled him with a sorrow he couldn't explain. He let the itch pass and sank back into a welcoming fatigue.

'You've talked about the rabbits.' Glenn said. 'But what about the island?'

'I've never seen the island.'

'You have in your dreams.'

'Actually I looked at it on Google Earth. It's what you'd expect a remote Scottish island to look like. Plain and grassy, some rocks, flowers, lots of dark blue sea. It looks pretty close to that in my dreams.'

'Do you feel sorry for the island and its people being threatened by the rabbits?'

'I find the story frightening. It's like cancer. It's like they removed the tumour – the rats – but then they find a lump – the rabbits – growing somewhere else, and it's too late.'

'But we know, rationally, it's not too late. There will be probably be some benefactor or grant that will cull or move the rabbits. No one is going to be murdered by them.'

'Of course. But then there'll be the next thing. A third animal.'

'Oh, there are always *problems*,' Glenn said. 'They'll get rid of the rabbits and then the rats might come back. Or there'll be too many sea eagles since they had more rabbits than they could eat. Or everyone might leave the island anyway because there's nothing to do and they're bored.'

'I know it's just nature,' Jeremy said.

'Not to you. Nature is pure threat. Disease. Suffering. The story and the dreams that come from it have meaning for you. You've never had a cancer scare, but recently you've had your own health issues – the heart stuff, taking medication for depression for the first time.'

Jeremy had nothing to say to this. Talking about the island seemed pointless, and he didn't like to remember the spate of doctor's appointments that had clouded the summer.

'Is the island beautiful in your dreams? Is it a happy place? Before it gets eaten away by the rabbits?'

'Very.'

'So worth a visit, then. In dreams.'

'When it's not a nightmare.'

'Is Marina there?'

'She was there once. But nothing happened. I just saw her there. Briefly.'

He woke again at eight. Thank God he'd snatched a few more hours. He was so tired these days. Tired to the point where he monitored sleep like a bank account. Marina was still asleep, and he stared at her face, willing her to wake. All he could think was that this might be the last time he would see it this close. Marina opened her eyes, blinked lazily and smiled at him. She stretched her arms up and then back down to prop her shoulders up against the pillows.

'So where did you go last night?'

'I didn't go anywhere,' Jeremy said. 'Where would I go?'

'I woke up and I thought you'd gone. But then I saw your clothes and shoes were still on the floor.'

'I probably went to the bathroom or something.'

'Or something.' Marina smiled. He couldn't catch her meaning.

'That's where I went. To the bathroom. There's nowhere else to go. This room doesn't even have a balcony. You were asleep by the time I came back.'

'You were in the bathroom for an hour.'

So she had been awake at least part of the night.

'Is everything OK?' Marina looked directly at him. It occurred to him that he'd never really seen the colour of her eyes. If someone had asked him previously what colour they were, he wouldn't have known what to say. He was always too dizzied by her to really take in the details. Now he saw they were the palest green. They reminded him of something, someone familiar. She was so blonde it was like a spotlight was permanently blanching her wide features, forever selecting her out. There was something of the moon about her face, a quality he'd never experienced in a woman he was attracted to before. Then he realised Glenn's eyes were the exact same shade, glowing brightly in a much darker face, worn with life, like rock pools in a desert. There are no other eyes I truly meet, he thought. Except the ones that frighten me the most.

'Everything's fine,' he said. 'I just want you.'

'I want you too.' she said.

'Now.'

She hesitated. He knew she was worried about running late. He rolled his body decisively over hers, and she giggled, but her eyes flickered with fear for a second as if she'd been captured. Once again he marvelled at the brightness of her body against the thick dark hair of his chest. He told her to turn round and raise her hips.

'I'm not used to being told what to do,' she said as she arched her back and dipped her shoulders, pushing her head into the pillow and her arse up into his crotch as he kneeled over her. 'But I'm enjoying it.'

They were hurried, but this time there was a momentum he had never experienced before with her. As he neared climax he heard the rustling again, and worry prickled over him but he ignored it and closed his eyes. Please don't ruin this, he thought. Marina's face was turned on the pillow but hidden under her long waves of white-blonde hair. He closed his eyes. His right hand slid over her back and down to her breast, the final thing he needed to get there. He was so close. Then he opened his eyes and there was a clang of metal against the floor and the rat, finally free from its prison, scrambled up the bed and streaked across the pillows, right over the outer ends of Marina's hair. Then it was gone. She hadn't even known it was there. He cried out in shock at the sight of it, and then he came. Marina made some noises that suggested the same thing, although he was never sure with her.

'I know, I know, I know,' he said. He sighed deeply.

'I know too,' she said, playing along in what he thought must be a game to her. 'I feel so good.'

He said it again. I know. They reached the end. He pulled out and lay down next to her.

'Oh my God,' she said. 'You.' She turned round and lay on her back and smiled brightly at him like they had just collided at a party and it was an unexpected pleasure. It saddened him instantly.

'I never took you for a talker,' she said.

'What do you mean?'

'Come on.' She smiled impishly. 'Just now. You said "I know" three times.'

'Oh. That. I don't know where that came from.'

'What is this thing you know, then? It was kind of weird what you were saying, but like, sexy-weird.'

'Oh, I don't know. It just came out.'

'People say all kinds of things in bed, don't they?' She spoke with a pragmatic air, and once again the sadness laid its hand on his shoulder. Then she peeled herself out of the bed and stretched. Standing, facing him, she buried her nose in her forearm and inhaled sharply.

'I smell like you,' she said.

He thought he would cry yet again. Instead, he said, 'Well, you have just been lying on top of me so you would smell like me, I suppose.'

'It's like being another person.'

He struggled to find words. And then gave up the struggle. He was physically and mentally spent. She began to dress, decided there wasn't time to wash. He watched her put on a beautiful emerald green shift dress with a sash and mango-yellow suede heels. He would never have put those two colours together, but now he saw they had an appealing lack of harmony, part of her unique eye. She was dousing herself with too much perfume, then she was picking up crumpled clothes and underwear off the floor and stuffing them into a plastic bag, talking about how she couldn't be late for her friend's wedding. Next she was putting on her earrings in the bathroom, rushing, she couldn't get the butterfly fastening onto the earring's metal spoke. What if, right now, he asked her what she had worn to her own wedding? She came back to the bed and said he could stay in the room as checkout wasn't until noon, and that she wanted to see him in a couple of weeks. They could do another weekend like this. After her trip to New York City. She went to fix her make up in the bathroom, and told him to stay in bed, get some more sleep.

In the weeks that came after that night in Oxfordshire with her, he wanted over and over to return to the time just before he and Marina had risen to the peak of their affair. That first month was like a physical space, a place that could be reclaimed at any time, made up of particular set pieces. His kitchen, so transformed with her there sitting at the solitary bar stool by the counter as he scrambled eggs for the two of them. The mediocre party where they had first met. The songs he had listened to after that night that would now always be associated with her, that she knew nothing about, songs he now couldn't bear to hear. But that world was a fiction, even though it was composed of real past events and places. In the end it was just a feeling of great expanse. It was rare to know instantly when a meeting or a moment was significant, and he had a habit of looking too hard for them. Yet there was still the desire to rewind, step into the expanse and have it all again, pick out those moments, even with the end in plain sight.

The rabbits were nowhere near that world. Far away they were digging, ripping through coffin wood, old rotten clothes and perhaps even skin and flesh, tunnelling through to the edge of the world. In the article he had read, they had dragged bones over the road like a pack of wild dogs. He didn't tell Glenn in the session that followed his hotel jaunt with Marina that he scoured the island for her in those dreams, searching for a flash of blonde hair moving across the mossy rocks and heather. In one dream he was searching so hard he didn't notice the real threat to the island – the relentless sea. The more he searched, the smaller the island got as the waves ate away at the coast. The rabbits were forced out of their holes by water, dragging anything to the surface they could find. Human remains, old and recent. But they couldn't beat the waves, the rocks eroding into sand like a fast-forwarded documentary. He heard a shout, caught a snatch of an unknown figure, and for a moment he thought it was Marina. He hurried round an immense rock and it revealed the figure to be Glenn. Glenn told him everything would be fine and that he wouldn't take his money. The rabbits were panicking, scrambling out of the water over and over each other. Soon they were like an island themselves, a clambering pile of the dead and the living, in the ever-swelling seawater.

He heard Marina repeat his name. He opened his eyes and realised she was right in front of him, standing over the bed. He saw concern in her face. My darling, he said. I'm sorry. I was miles away.

She gave him the gentlest smile. 'You had your eyes closed and the most perplexed expression on your face. You were thinking about those rabbits and that crazy island, weren't you?' she said.

'Yes,' he said, glad it could be the truth.

Next time he would confront her. He was certain of that.

Acknowledgements

I would like to give my grateful acknowledgement to the following publications in which the stories first appeared:
'Imposters' in *the Dublin Review*
'Derma' in the *Erotic Review*
'The Real Beast' in *Prole* Books Issue 14
'Only the Visible Can Vanish' in *The Wells Street Journal*
'The Eight' in *The Bitter Oleander*
'What Have I To Do With You?' in the *Erotic Review*
'Baked' in the *Erotic Review*
'Playing House' on Storgy.com

Thank you also to my crucial first readers: Jessie Pay, Charlotte Ginsborg, Mary Green, Kira Jolliffe, Mike Delwiche and my parents, Carol Martin-Sperry and Michael Maconochie.

Others I'd like to thank in particular are Helen Gordon for her advice, and for helping me bring 'What Have I To Do With You?' and 'Only the Visible Can Vanish' into fruition, and the *Erotic Review* for publishing my first two finished stories.

Thank you to Martin Yong and Colin Taylor for their help with the development of the cover design.

Cultured Llama Publishing
Poems | Stories | Curious Things

Cultured Llama was born in a converted stable. This creature of humble birth drank greedily from the creative source of the poets, writers, artists and musicians that visited, and soon the llama fulfilled the destiny of its given name.

Cultured Llama aspires to quality from the first creative thought through to the finished product.

www.culturedllama.co.uk

Also published by Cultured Llama

Poetry

strange fruits by Maria C. McCarthy
Paperback; 72pp; 203×127mm; 978-0-9568921-0-2; July 2011

A Radiance by Bethany W. Pope
Paperback; 70pp; 203×127mm; 978-0-9568921-3-3; June 2012

The Strangest Thankyou by Richard Thomas
Paperback; 98pp; 203×127mm; 978-0-9568921-5-7; November 2012

The Night My Sister Went to Hollywood by Hilda Sheehan
Paperback; 82pp; 203×127mm; 978-0-9568921-8-8; March 2013

Notes from a Bright Field by Rose Cook
Paperback; 104pp; 203×127mm; 978-0-9568921-9-5; July 2013

Sounds of the Real World by Gordon Meade
Paperback; 104pp; 203×127mm; 978-0-9926485-0-3; August 2013

The Fire in Me Now by Michael Curtis
Paperback; 90pp; 203×127mm; 978-0-9926485-4-1; August 2014

Short of Breath by Vivien Jones
Paperback; 102pp; 203×127mm; 978-0-9926485-5-8; October 2014

Cold Light of Morning by Julian Colton
Paperback; 90pp; 203×127mm; 978-0-9926485-7-2; March 2015

Automatic Writing by John Brewster
Paperback; 96pp; 203×127mm; 978-0-9926485-8-9; July 2015

Zygote Poems by Richard Thomas
Paperback; 66pp; 178×127mm; 978-0-9932119-5-9; July 2015

Les Animots: A Human Bestiary by Gordon Meade, images by Douglas Robertson
Hardback; 166pp; 203×127mm; 978-0-9926485-9-6; December 2015

Memorandum: Poems for the Fallen by Vanessa Gebbie
Paperback; 90pp; 203×127mm; 978-0-9932119-4-2; February 2016

The Light Box by Rosie Jackson
Paperback; 108pp; 203×127mm; 978-0-9932119-7-3; March 2016

There Are No Foreign Lands by Mark Holihan
Paperback; 96pp; 203×127mm; 978-0-9932119-8-0; June 2016

Short stories

Canterbury Tales on a Cockcrow Morning by Maggie Harris
Paperback; 138pp; 203×127mm; 978-0-9568921-6-4; September 2012

As Long as it Takes by Maria C. McCarthy
Paperback; 168pp; 203×127mm; 978-0-9926485-1-0; February 2014

In Margate by Lunchtime by Maggie Harris
Paperback; 204pp; 203×127mm; 978-0-9926485-3-4; February 2015

The Lost of Syros by Emma Timpany
Paperback; 128pp; 203×127mm; 978-0-9932119-2-8; July 2015

Curious things

Digging Up Paradise: Potatoes, People and Poetry in the Garden of England by Sarah Salway
Paperback; 164pp; 203×203mm; 978-0-9926485-6-5; June 2014

Punk Rock People Management: A No-Nonsense Guide to Hiring, Inspiring and Firing Staff by Peter Cook
Paperback; 40pp; 210×148mm; 978-0-9932119-0-4; February 2015

Do it Yourself: A History of Music in Medway by Stephen H. Morris
Paperback; 504pp; 229×152mm; 978-0-9926485-2-7; April 2015

The Music of Business: Business Excellence Fused with Music by Peter Cook – NEW EDITION
Paperback; 318pp; 210×148mm; 978-0-9932119-1-1; May 2015

The Hungry Writer by Lynne Rees
Paperback; 246pp; 244×170mm; 978-0-9932119-3-5; September 2015

The Ecology of Everyday Things by Mark Everard
Hardback; 126pp; 216×140mm; 978-0-9932119-6-6; November 2015

Lightning Source UK Ltd.
Milton Keynes UK
UKOW02f1046280916

283997UK00002B/4/P